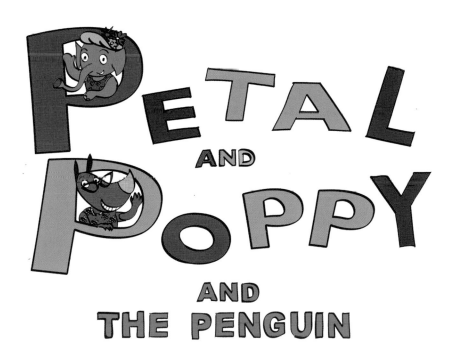

PETAL AND POPPY

AND THE PENGUIN

For information about permission to reproduce selections from this
book, write to Permissions, Houghton Mifflin Harcourt Publishing
Company, 215 Park Avenue South, New York, New York 10003.

www.hmhbooks.com

The text of this book is set in Cheltenham.
The display type was hand-lettered.
The illustrations were created digitally.

The Library of Congress Cataloging-in-Publication Data
Jahn-Clough, Lisa.
Petal and Poppy and the penguin / by Lisa Clough and Ed Briant.
p. cm.
Summary: Best friends Petal, the tuba-playing elephant, and Poppy,
the adventurous rhinoceros, have very different reactions when
they discover a penguin in their garden one stormy day.
ISBN 978-0-544-13330-3 paperback
ISBN 978-0-544-13770-7 paper over board
[1. Best friends—Fiction. 2. Friendship—Fiction. 3. Elephants—
Fiction. 4. Rhinoceroses—Fiction. 5. Penguins—Fiction.] I. Briant,
Ed, illustrator. II. Title.
PZ7.J153536Pfp 2014
[E]—dc23
2013020668

Manufactured in China
SCP 10 9 8 7 6 5 4 3 2 1

4500451496

Petal and Poppy and the Penguin

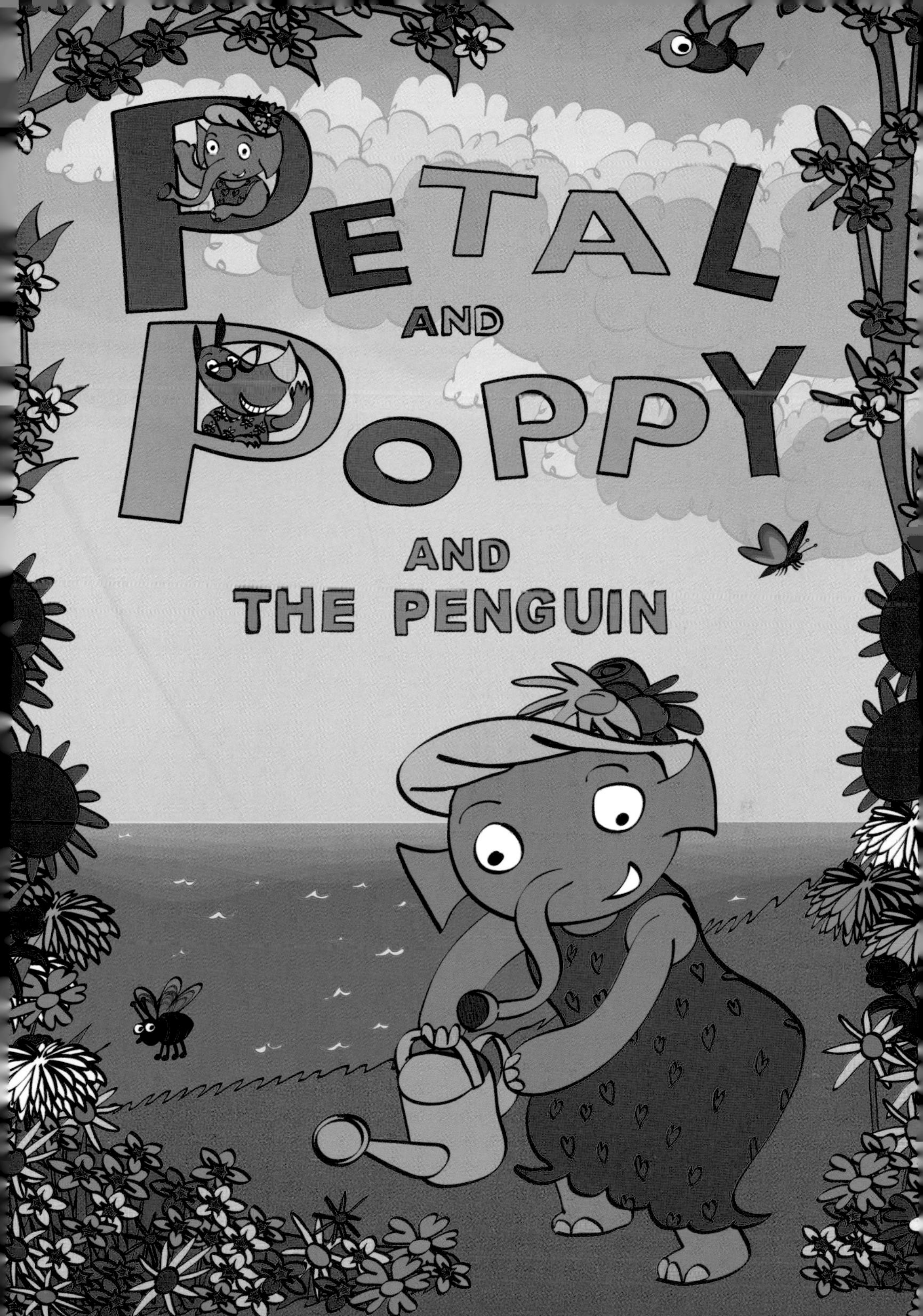

By Lisa Clough and Ed Briant

Houghton Mifflin Harcourt
Boston New York

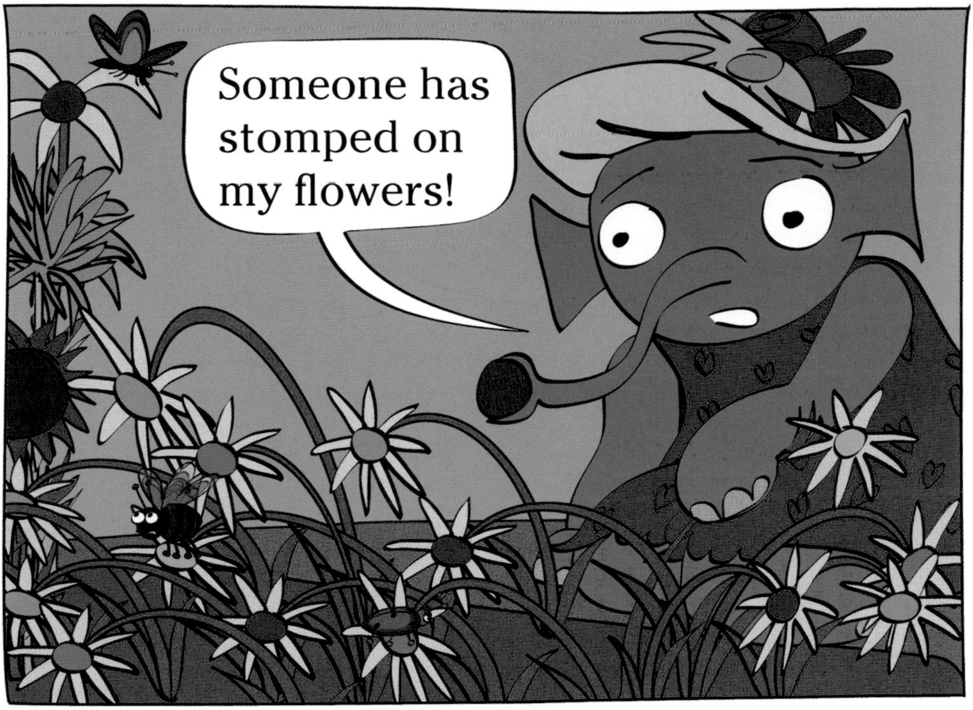
Someone has stomped on my flowers!

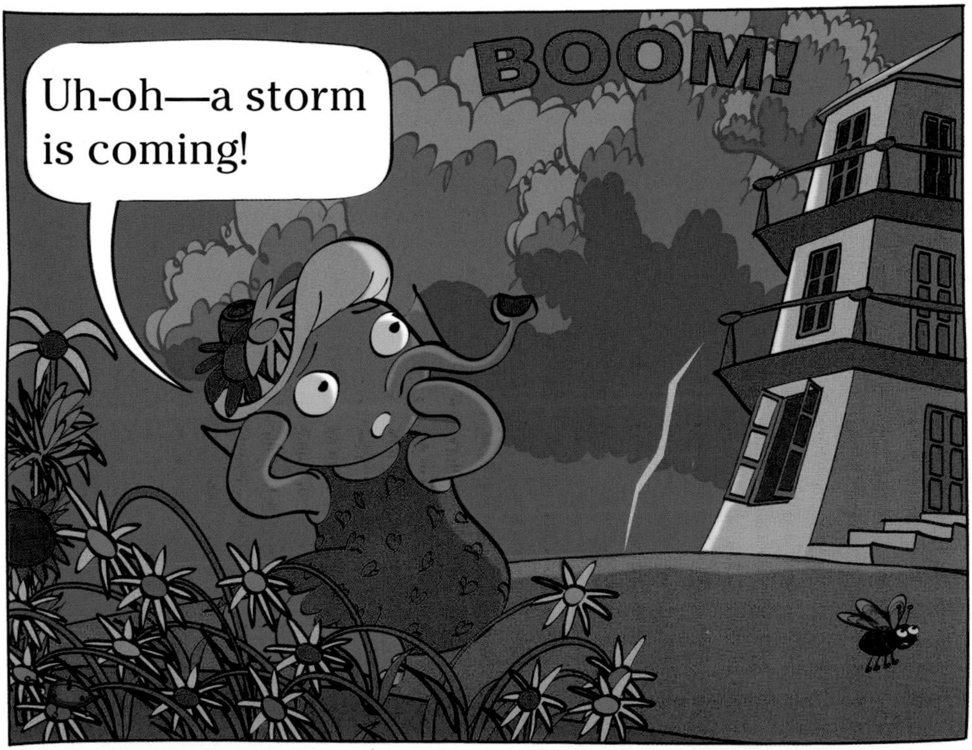
Uh-oh—a storm is coming!
BOOM!

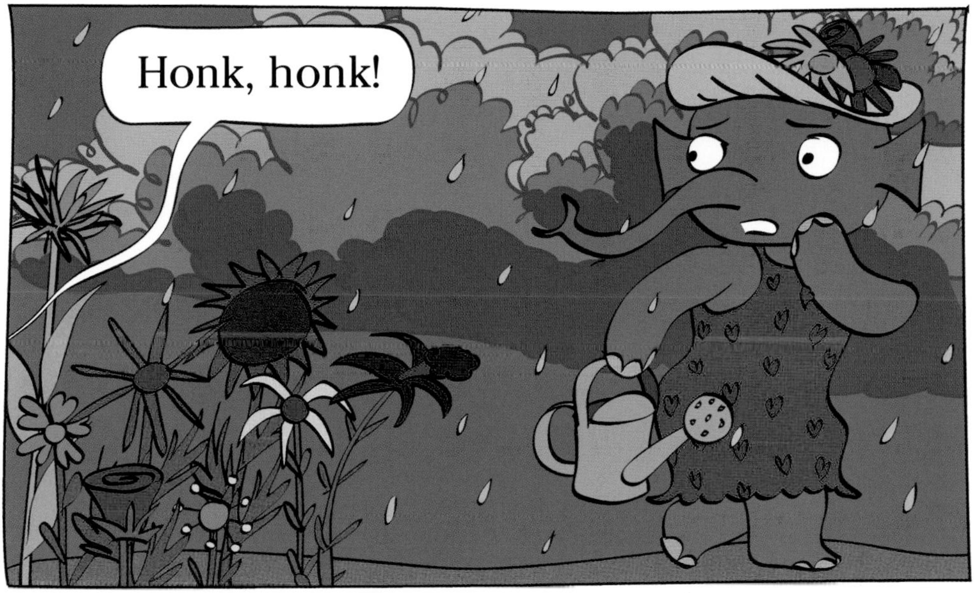
Honk, honk!

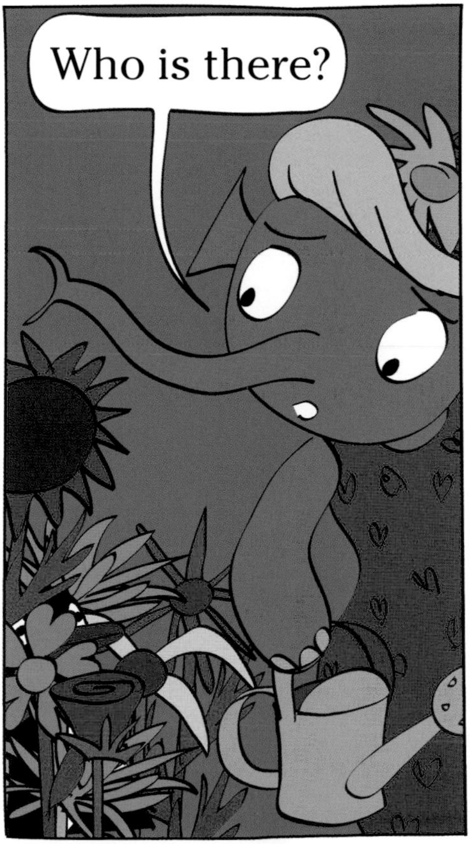
Who is there?

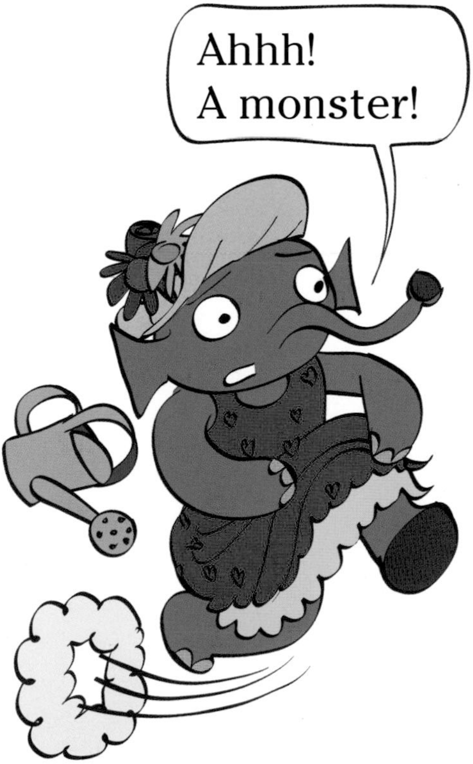
Ahhh!
A monster!

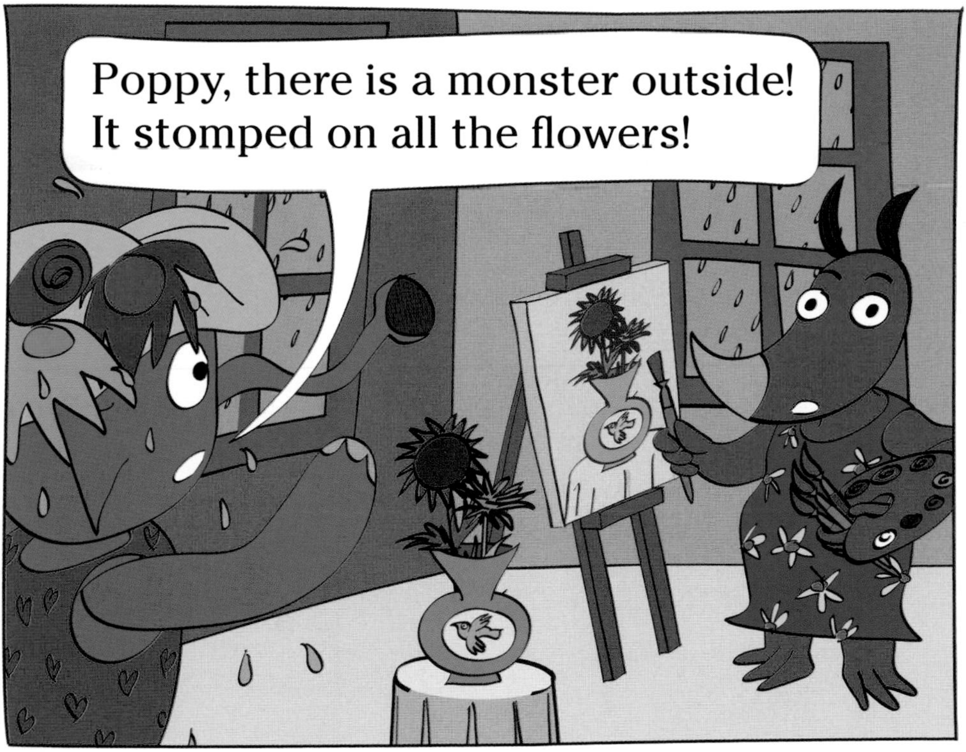
Poppy, there is a monster outside!
It stomped on all the flowers!

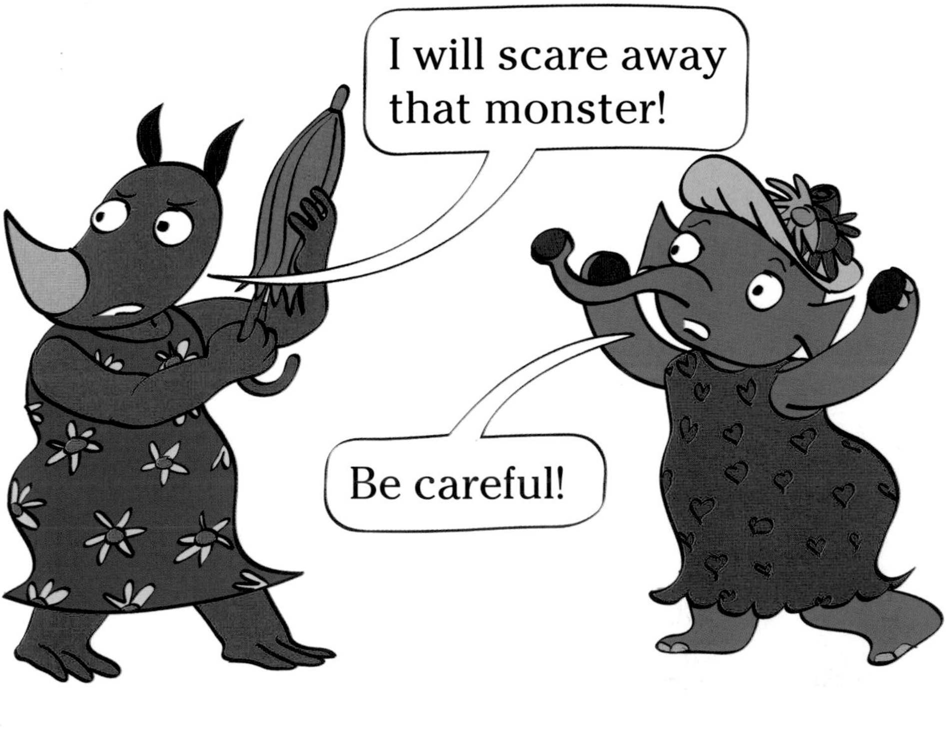
I will scare away
that monster!
Be careful!

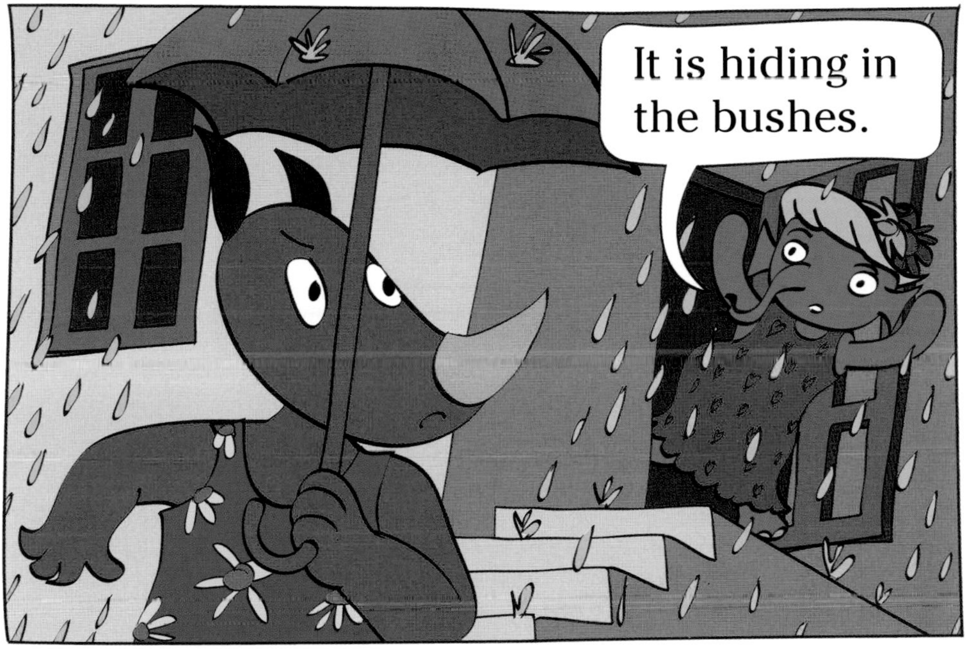
It is hiding in the bushes.

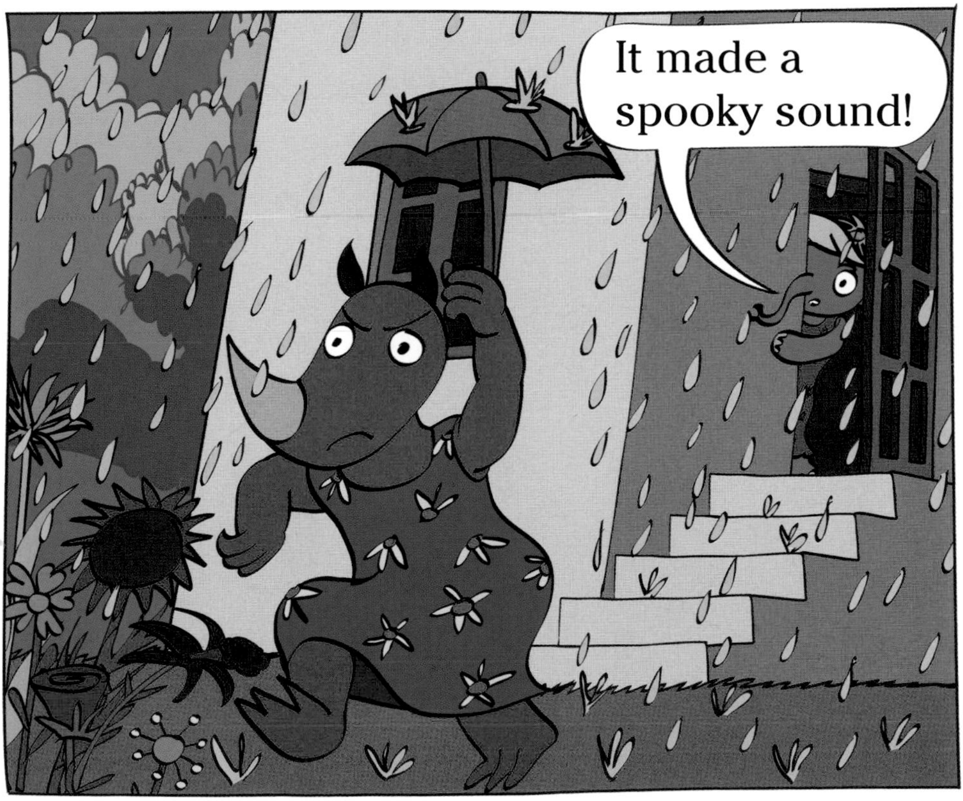
It made a spooky sound!

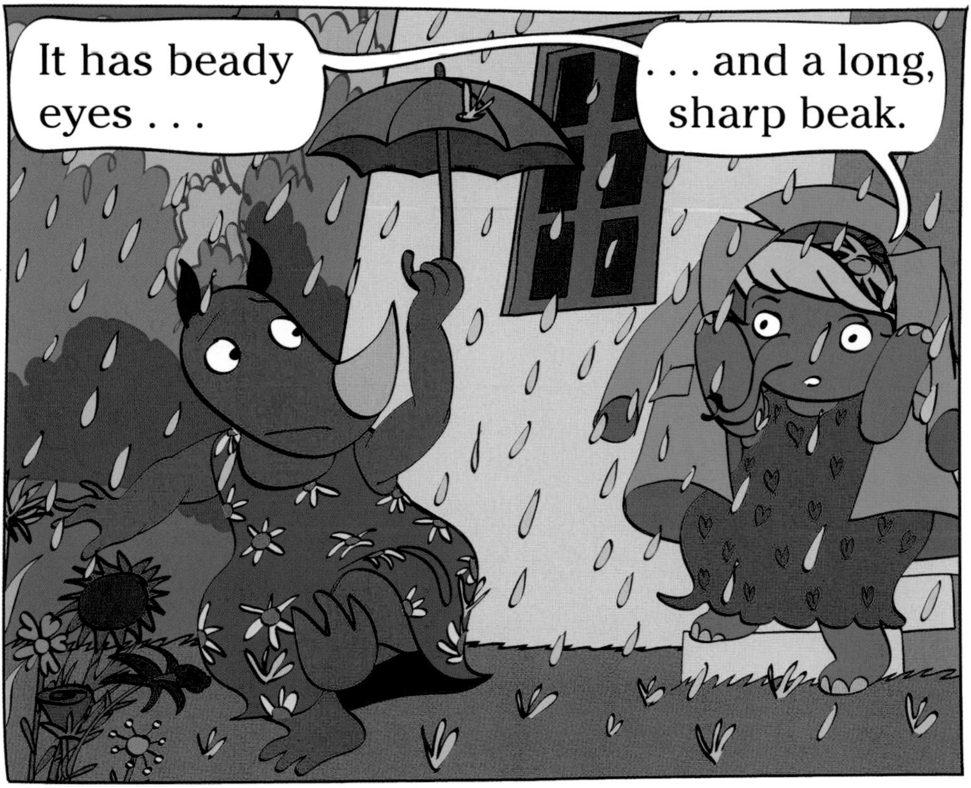
It has beady eyes . . .
. . . and a long, sharp beak.

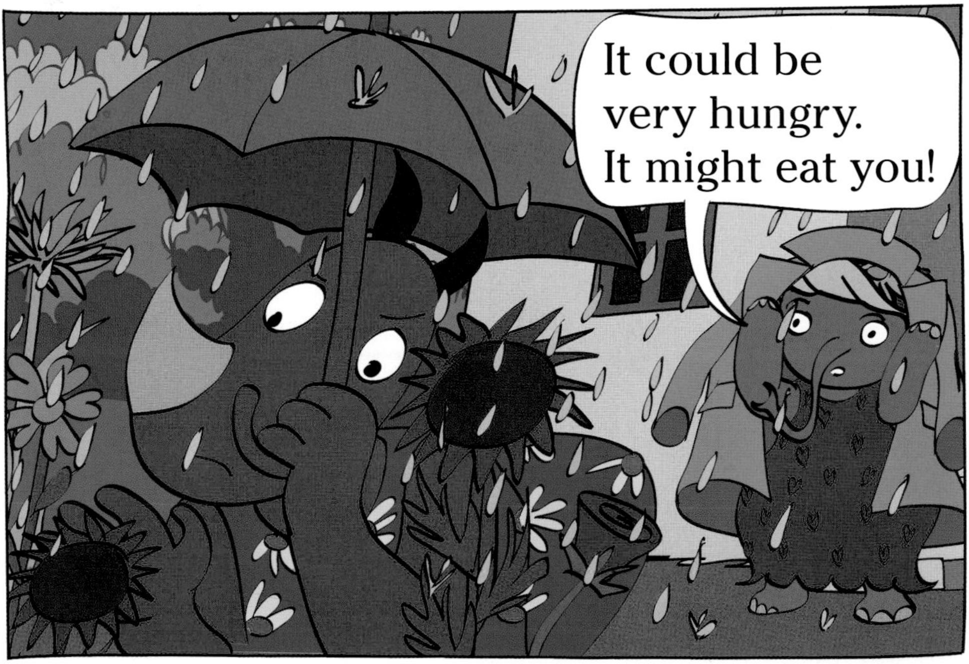
It could be very hungry. It might eat you!

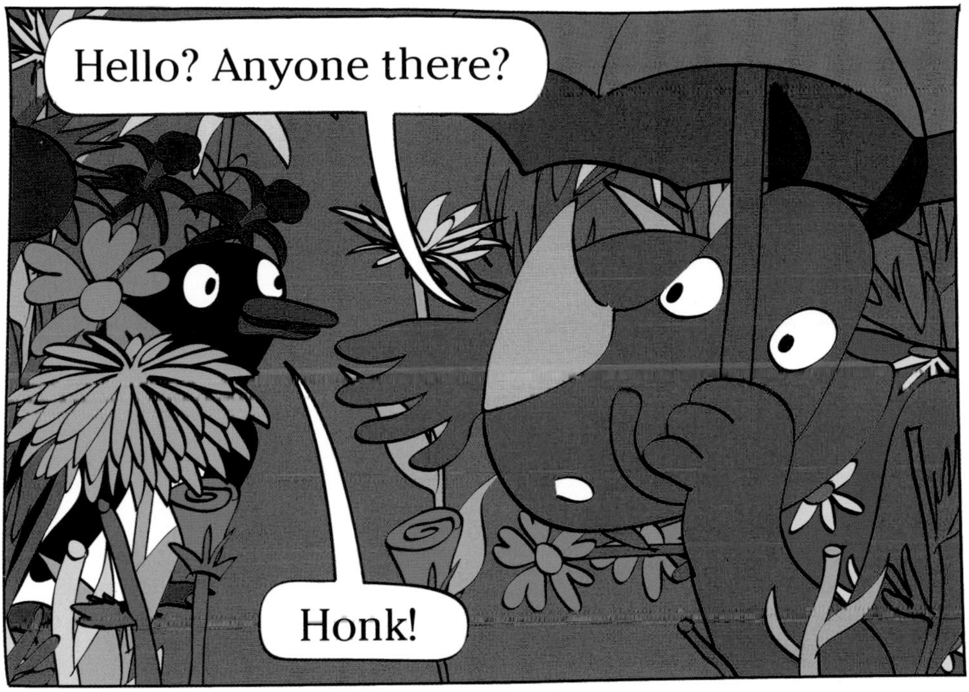
Hello? Anyone there?
Honk!

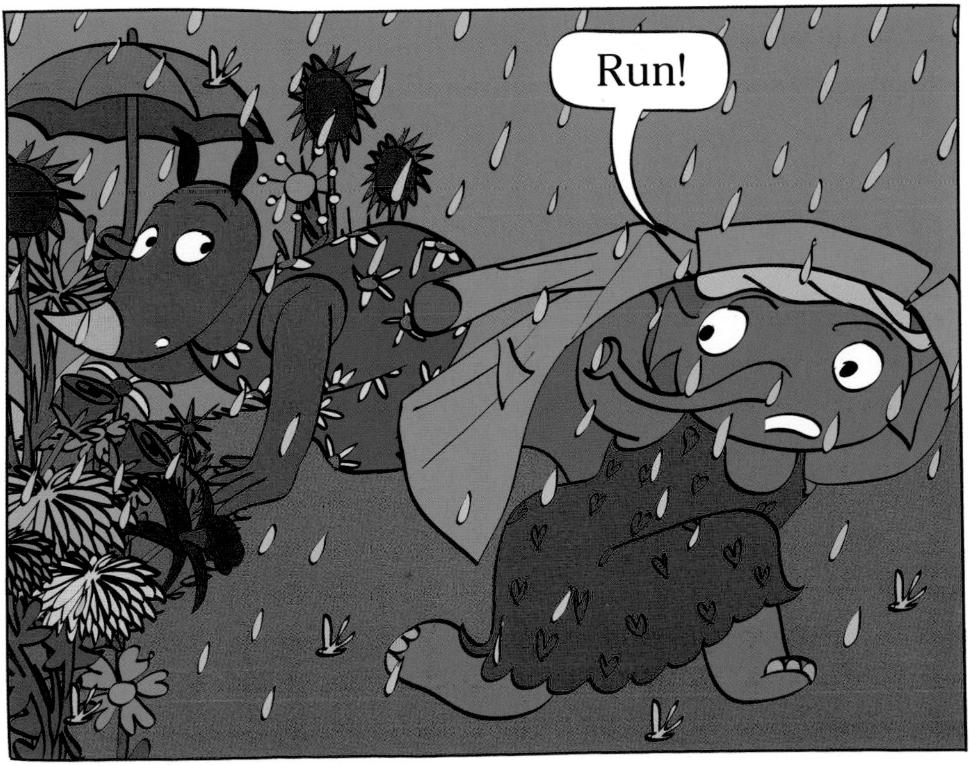
Run!

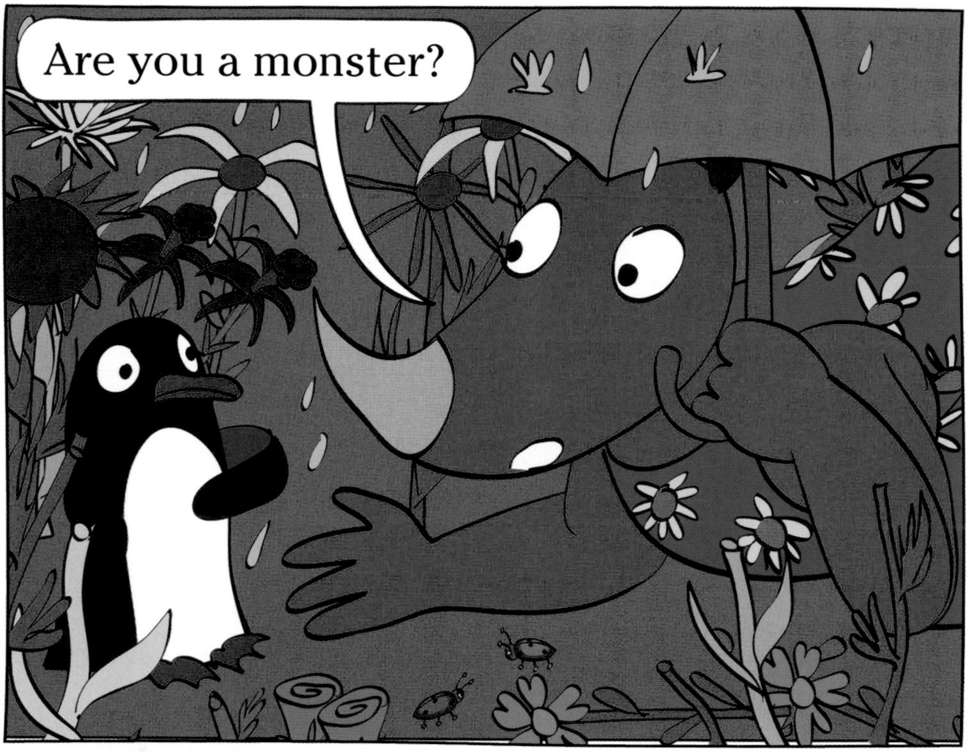
Are you a monster?

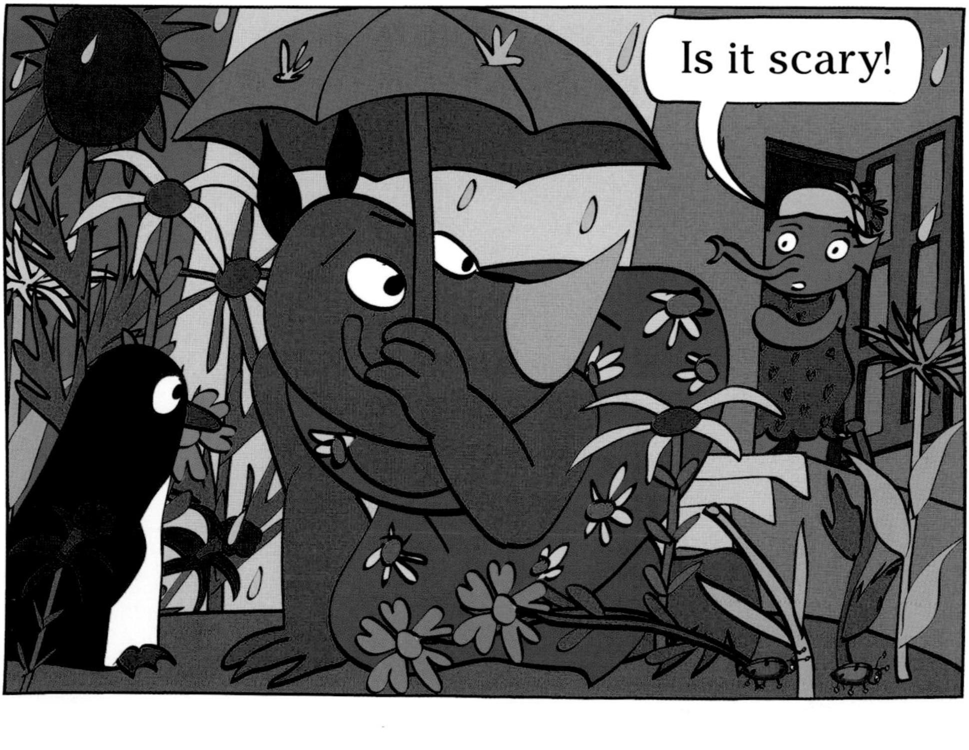
Is it scary!

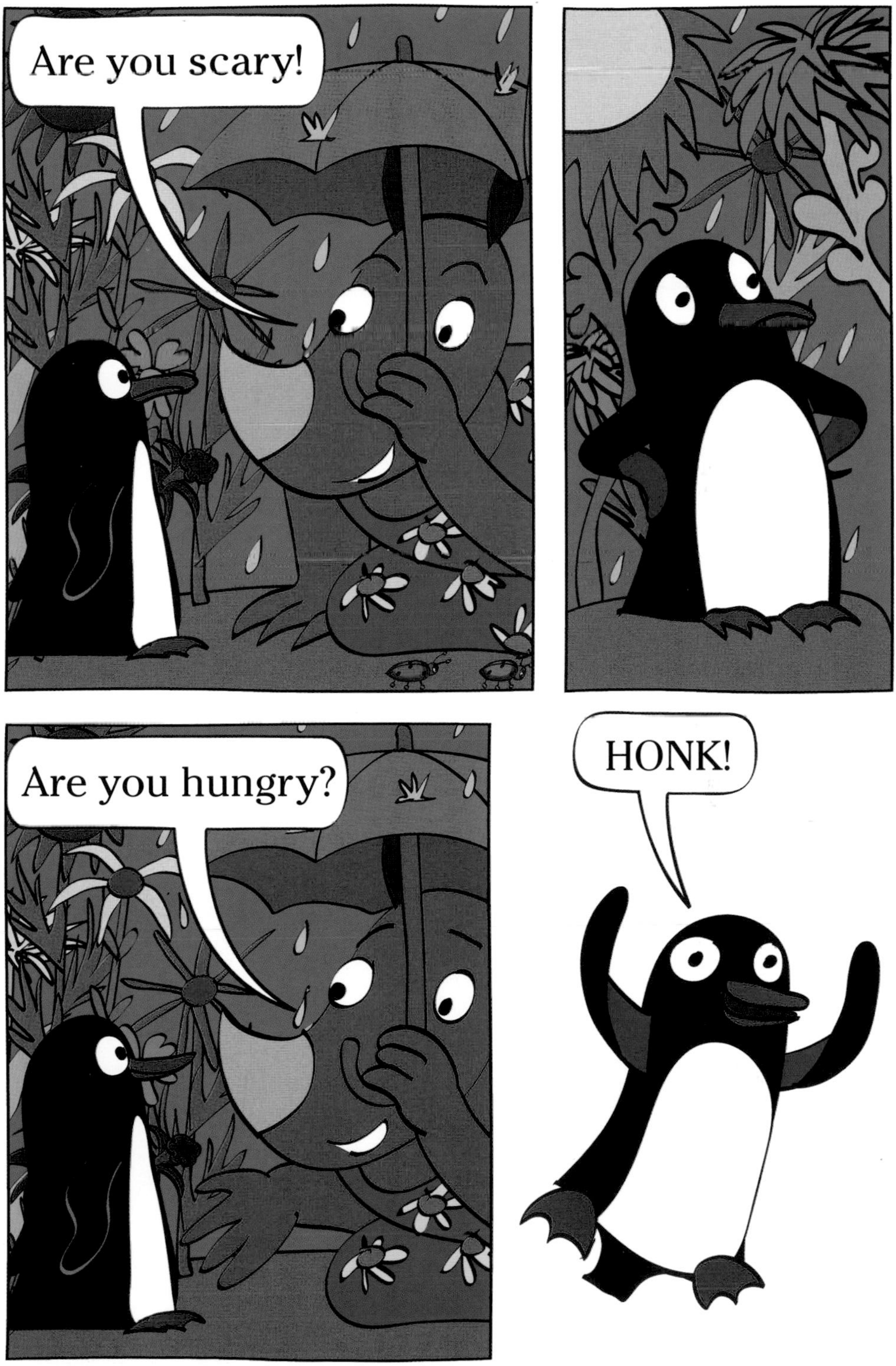
Are you scary!
Are you hungry?
HONK!

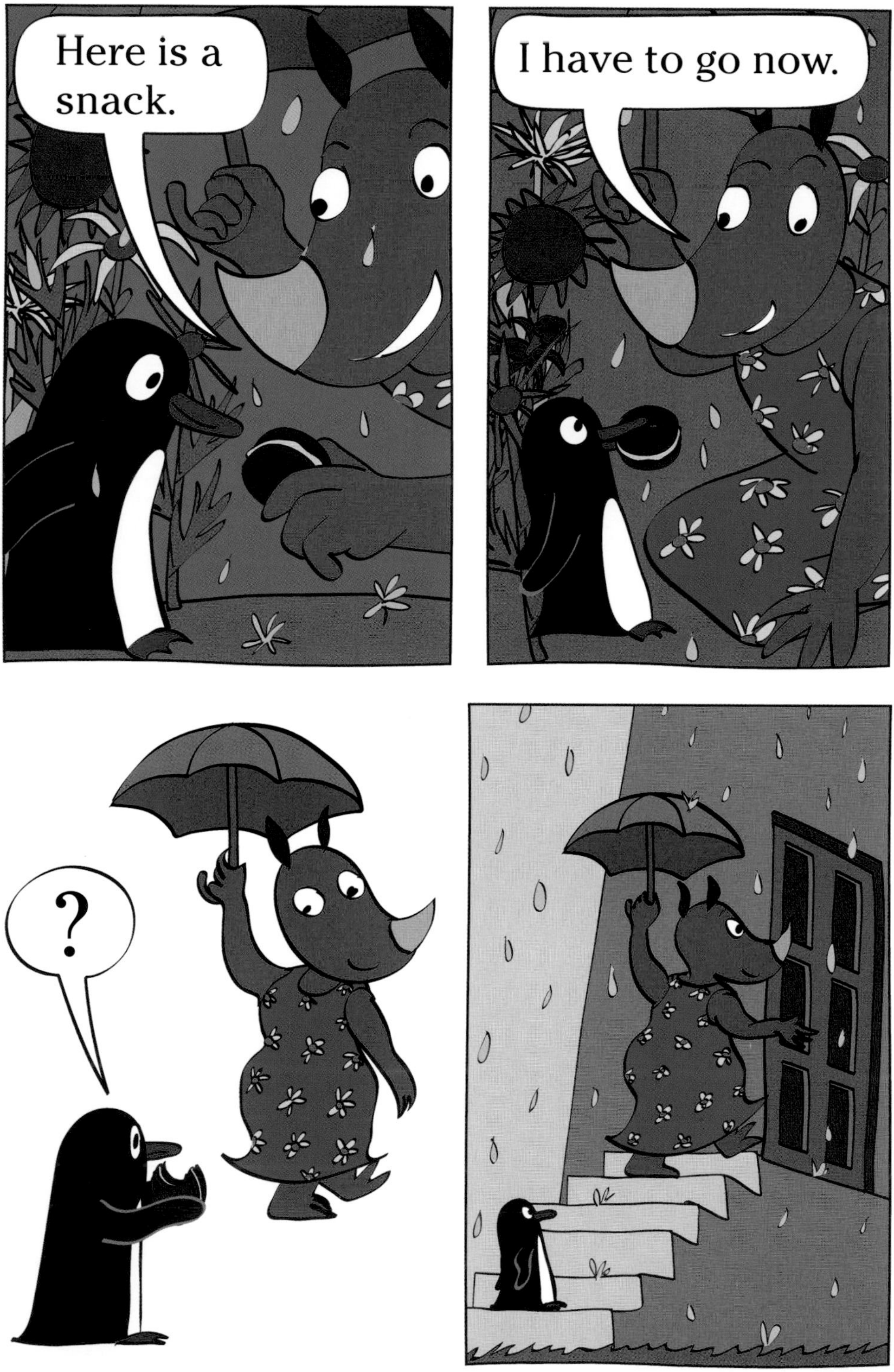
Here is a snack.
I have to go now.
?

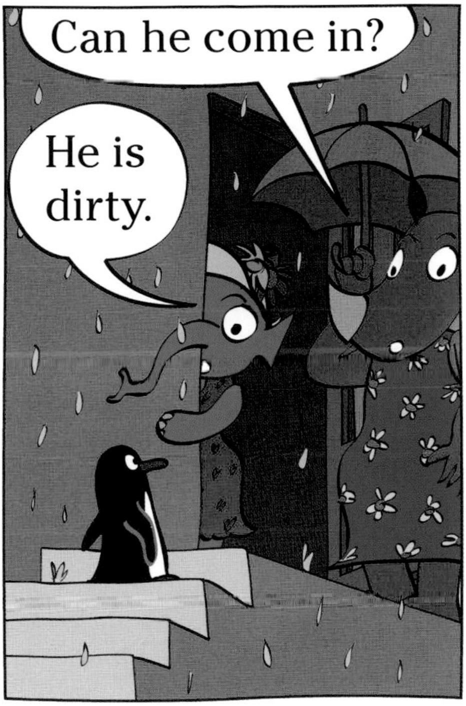
Can he come in?
He is dirty.

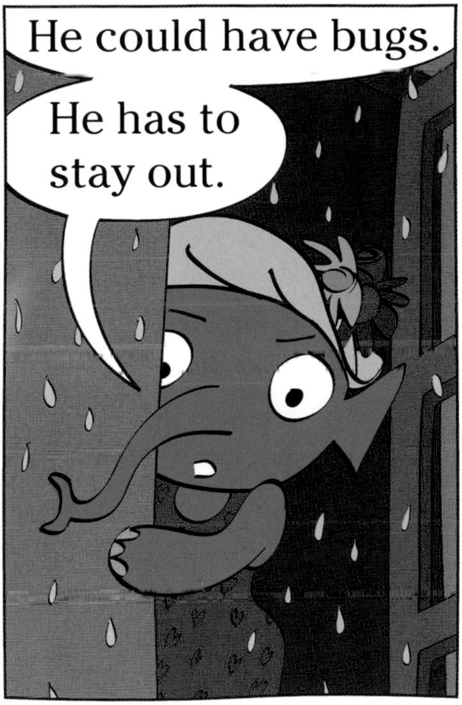
He could have bugs.
He has to stay out.

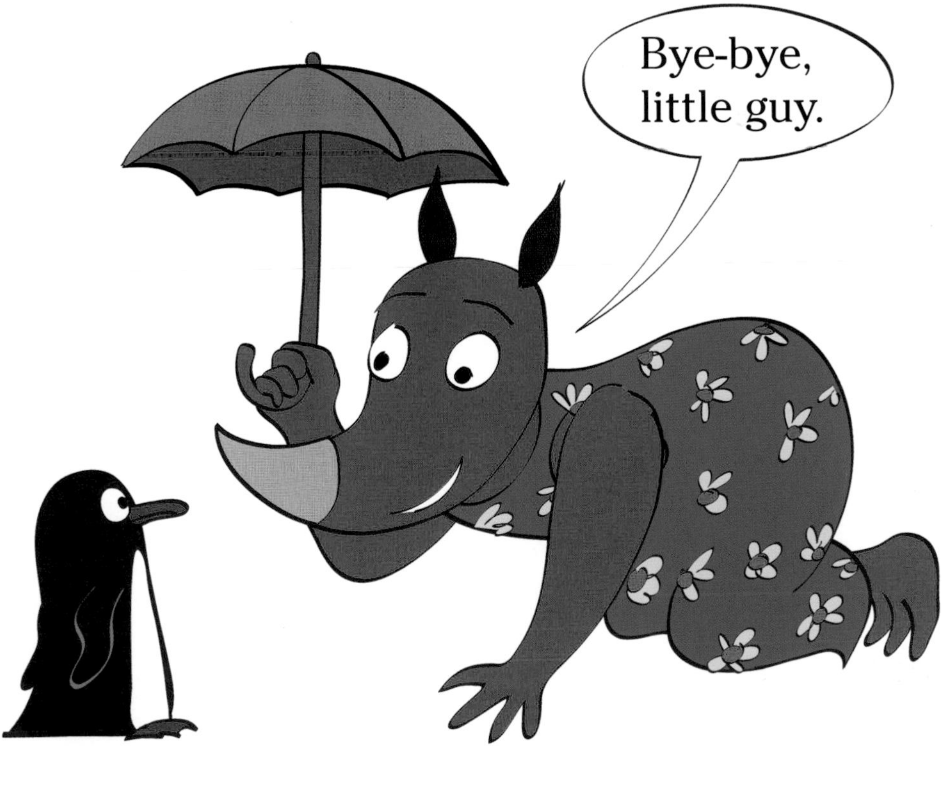
Bye-bye, little guy.

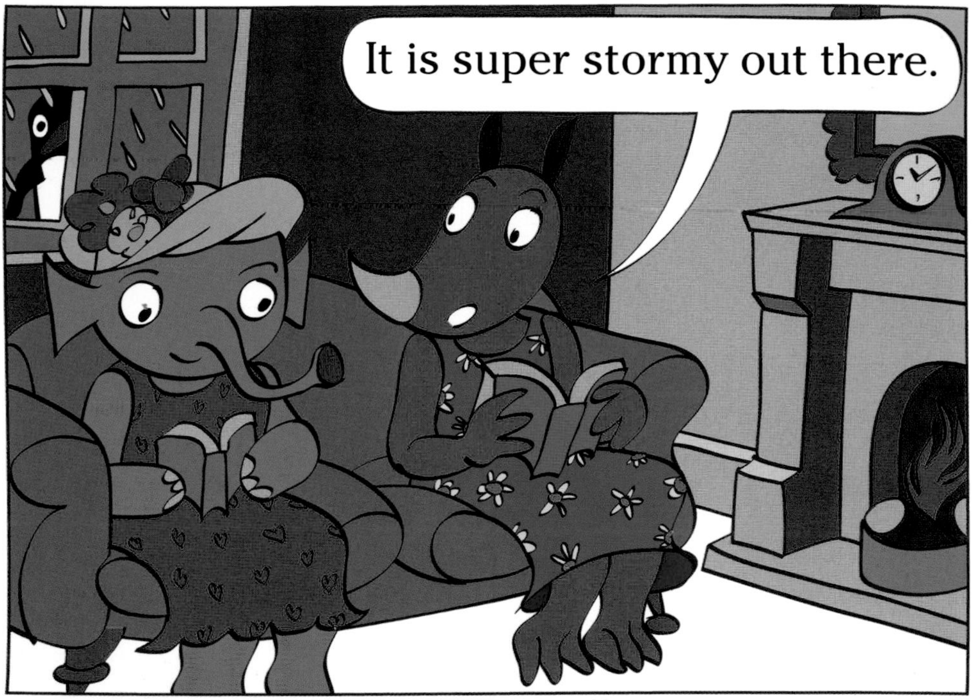
It is super stormy out there.

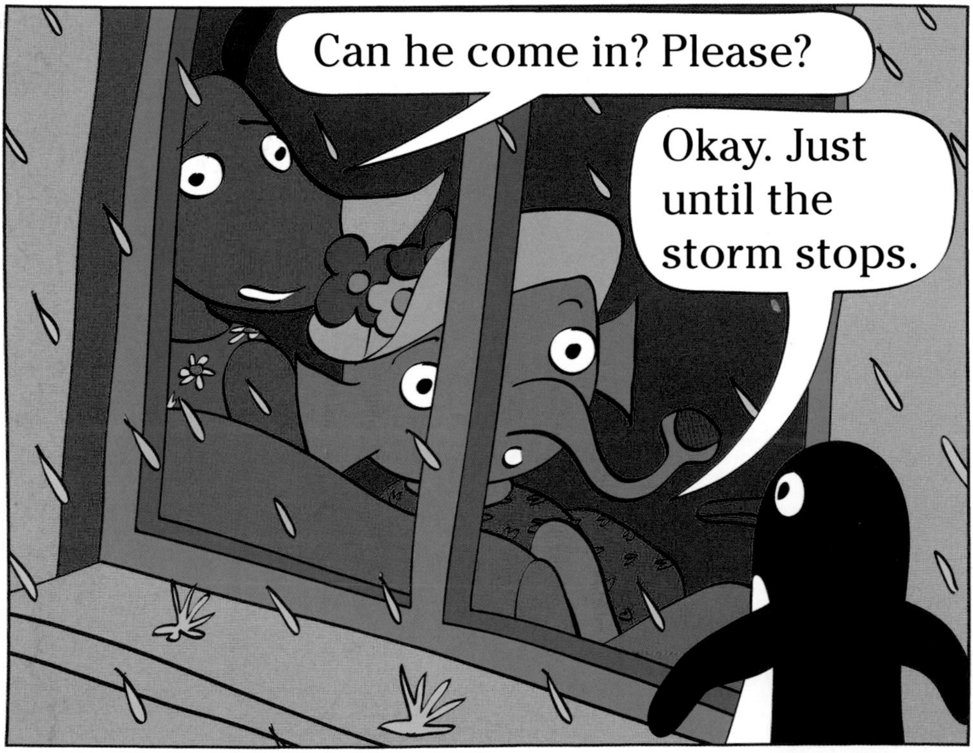
Can he come in? Please?
Okay. Just until the storm stops.

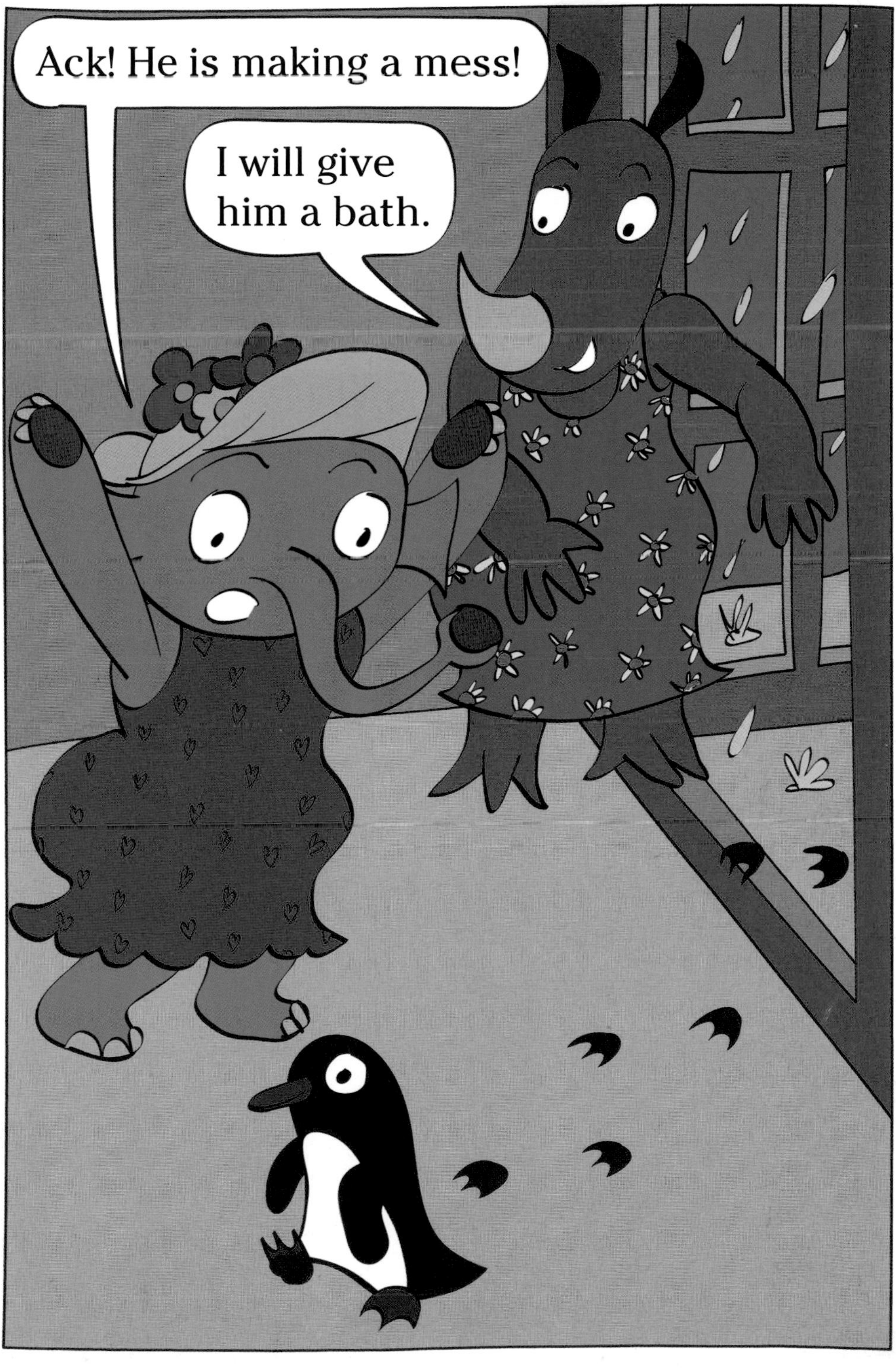
Ack! He is making a mess!
I will give him a bath.

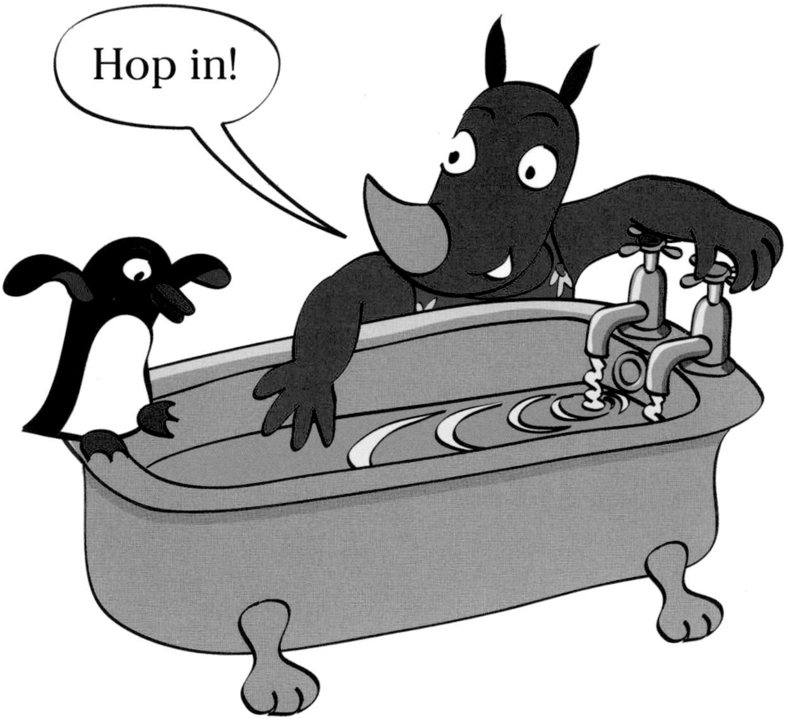
Hop in!

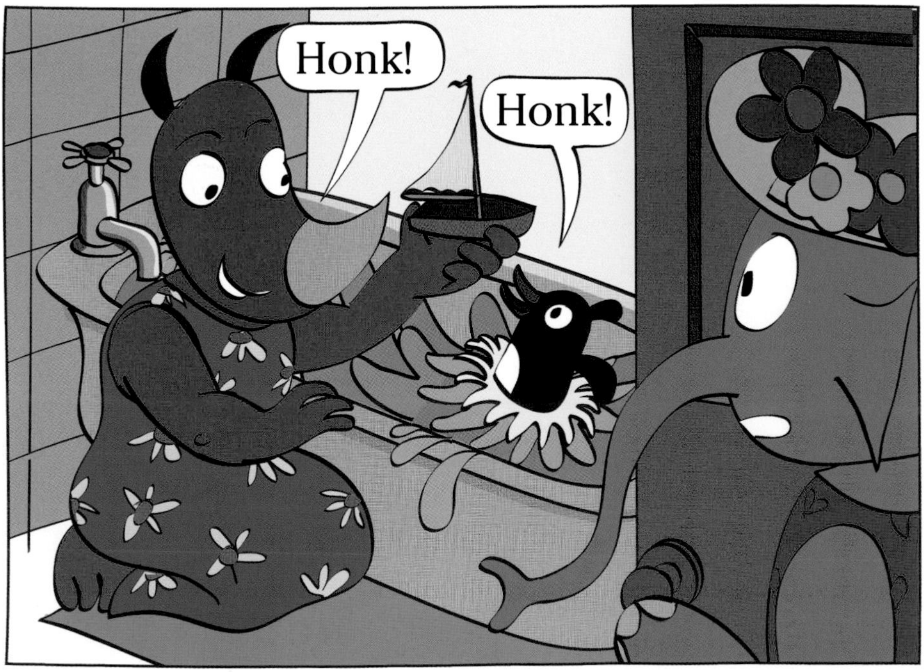
Honk!
Honk!

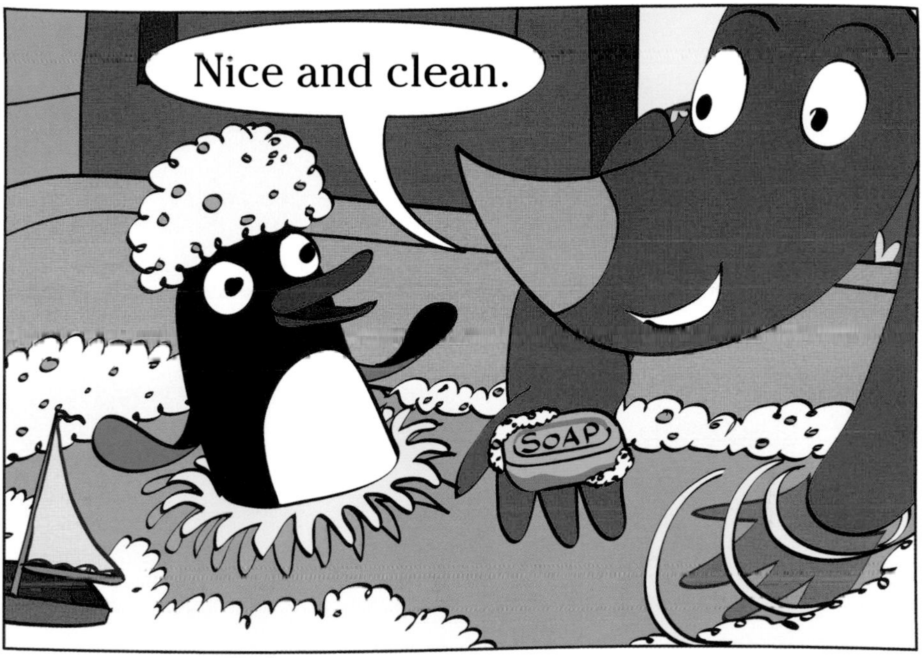
Nice and clean.
SOAP

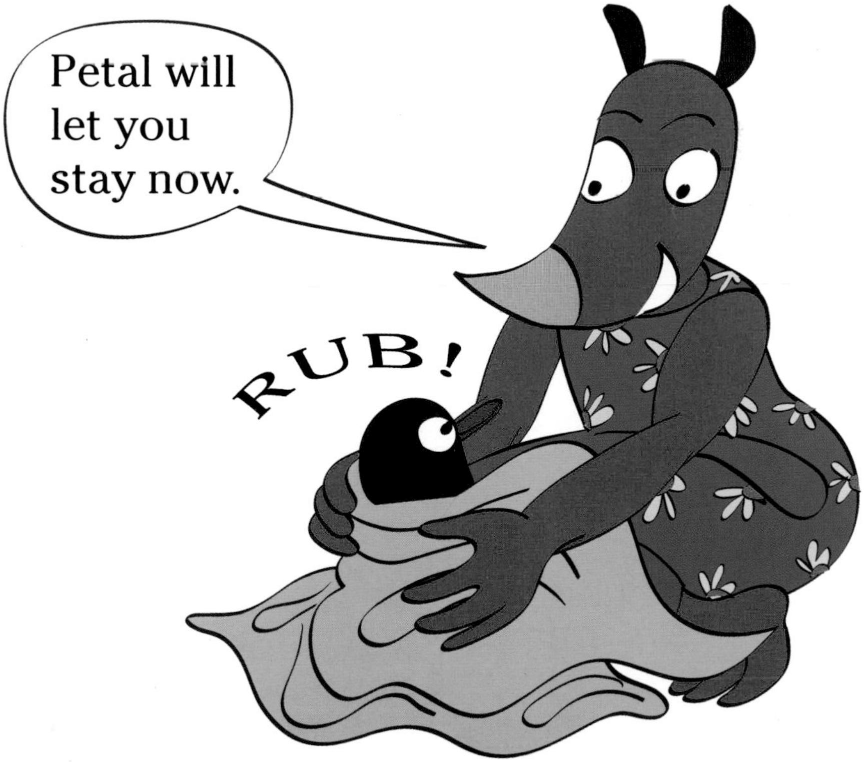
Petal will let you stay now.
RUB!

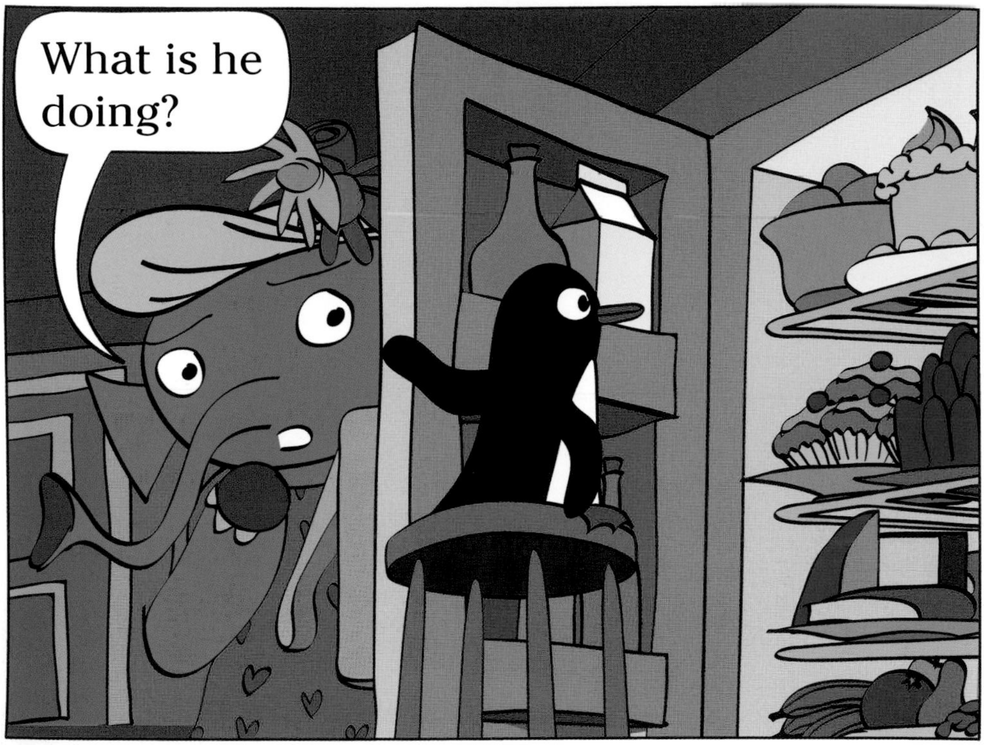
What is he doing?

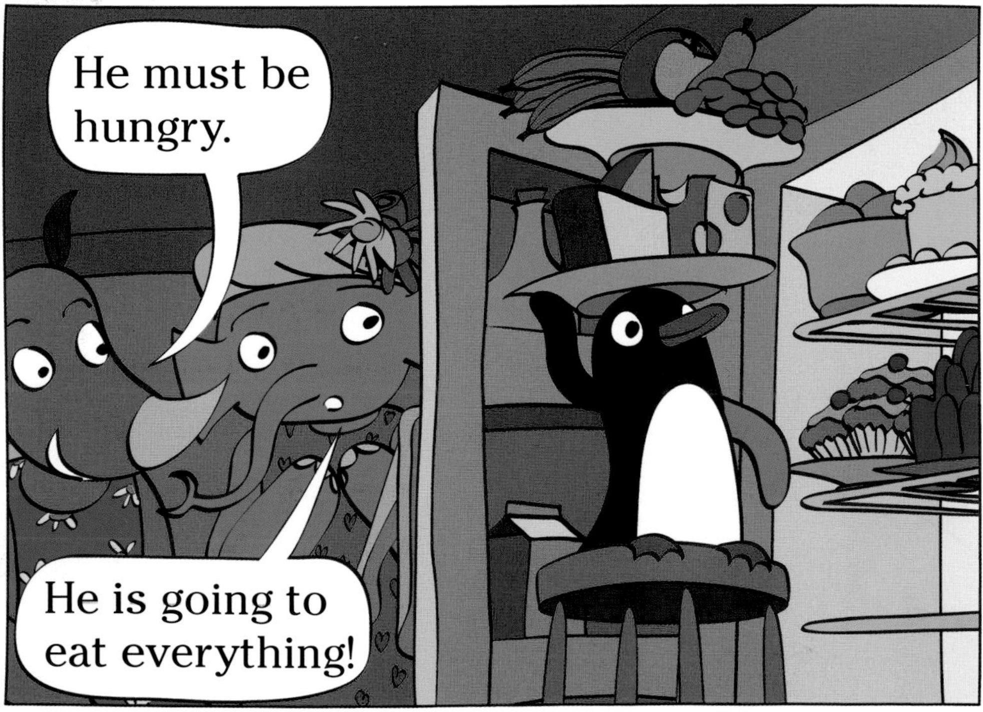
He must be hungry.
He is going to eat everything!

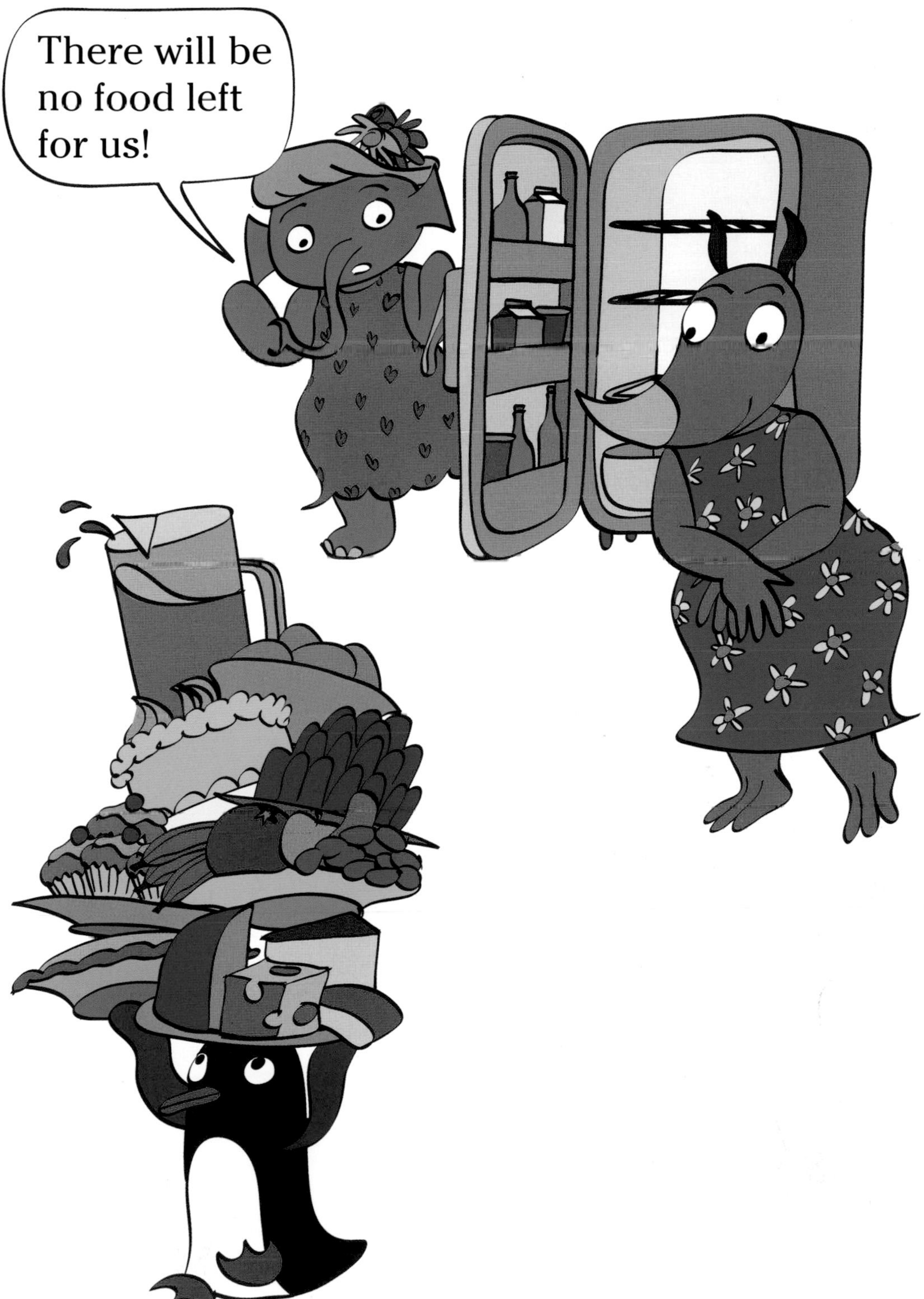
There will be no food left for us!

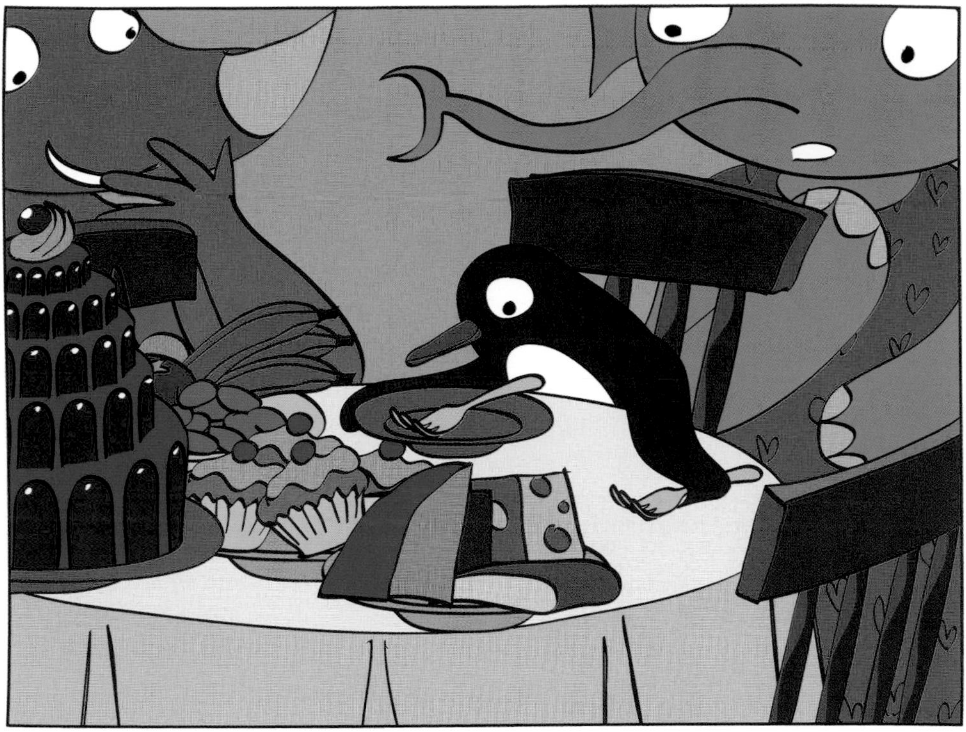

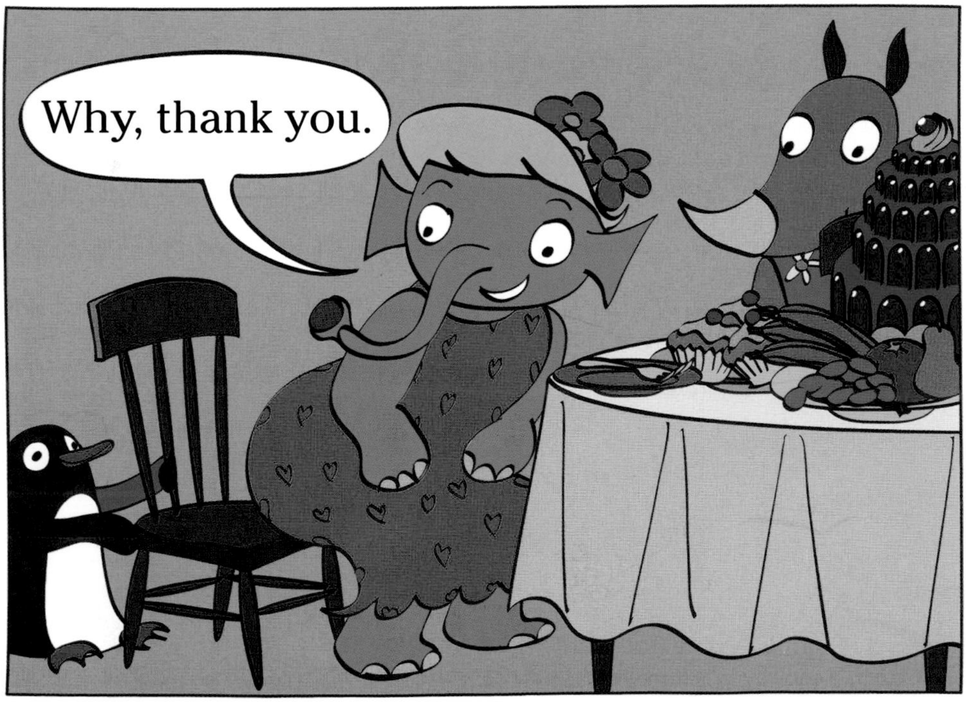
Why, thank you.

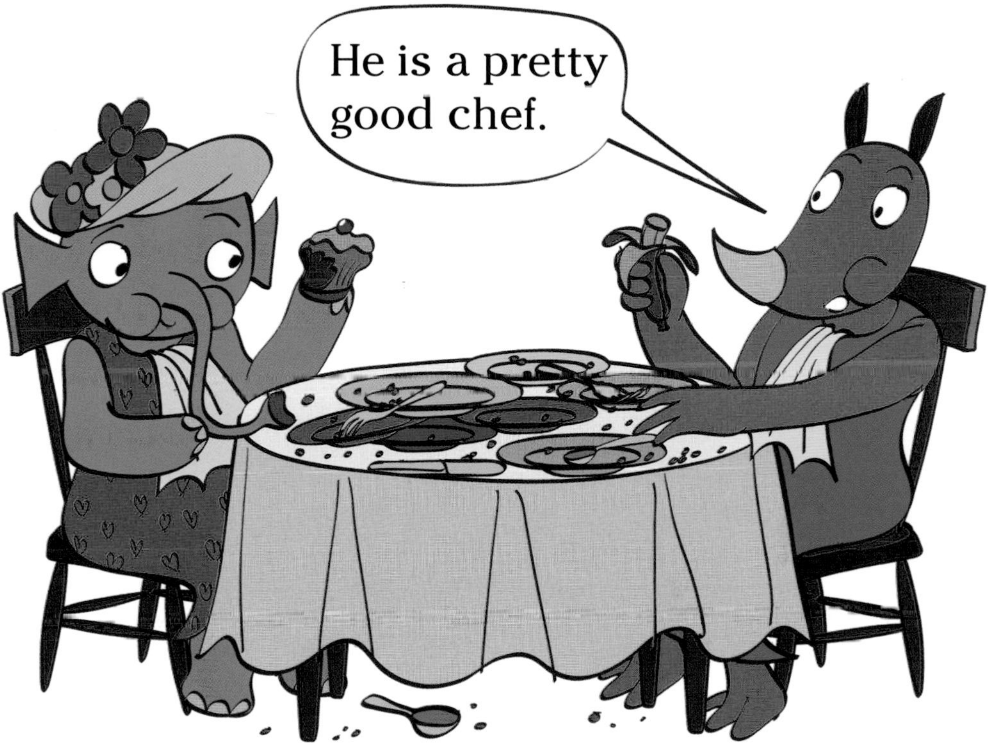
He is a pretty
good chef.

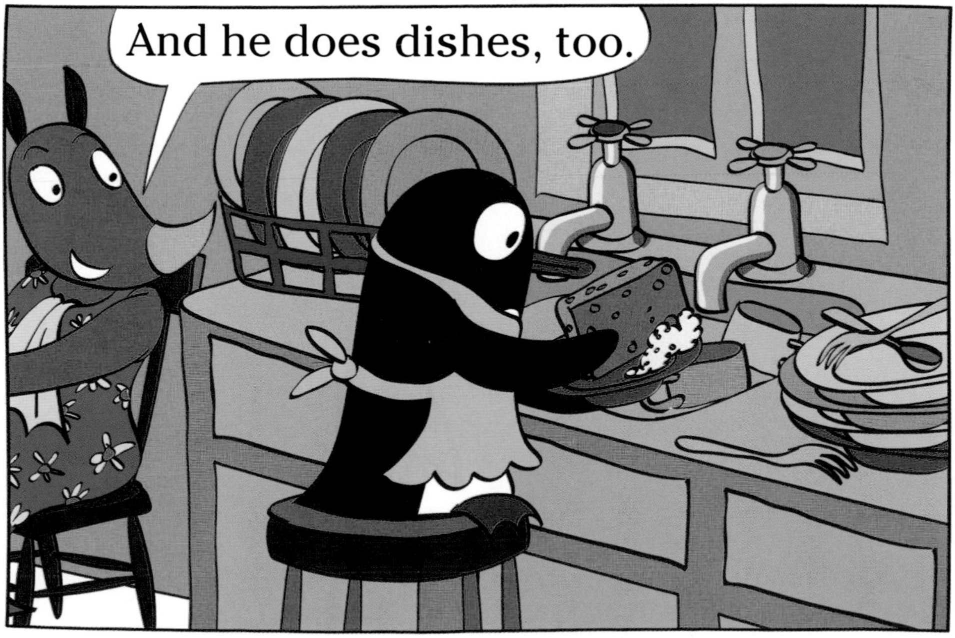
And he does dishes, too.

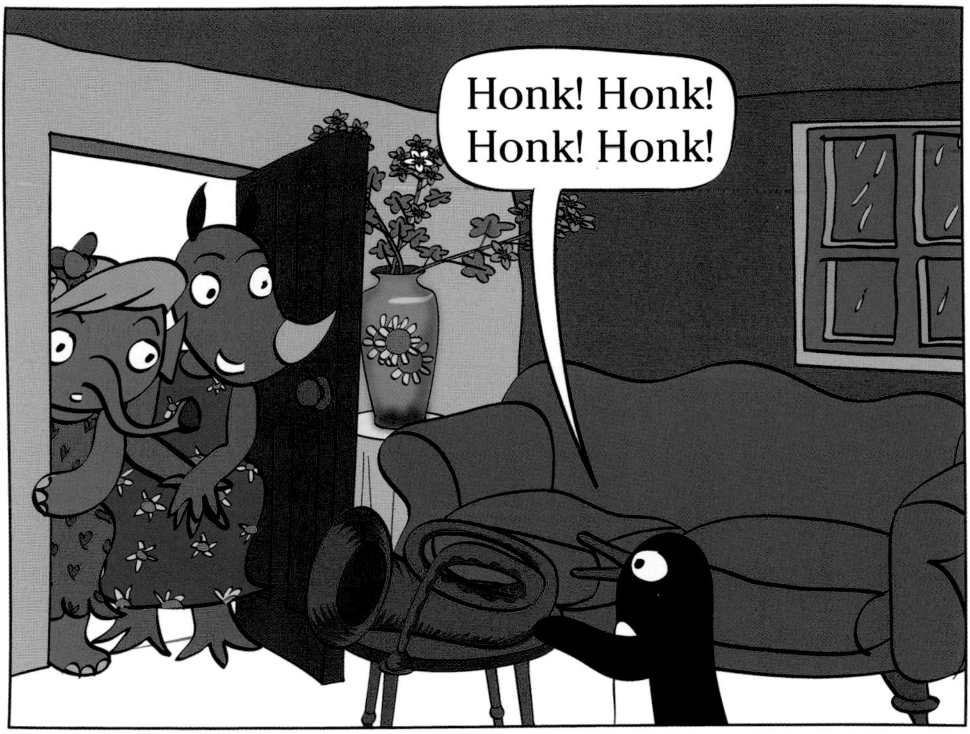
Honk! Honk!
Honk! Honk!

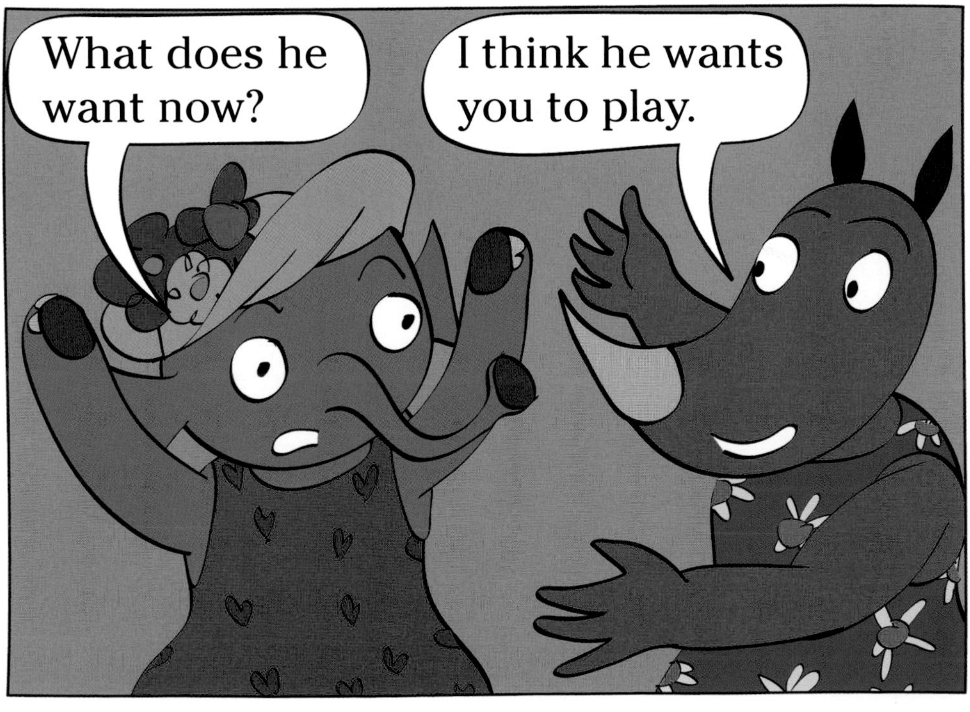
What does he
want now?
I think he wants
you to play.

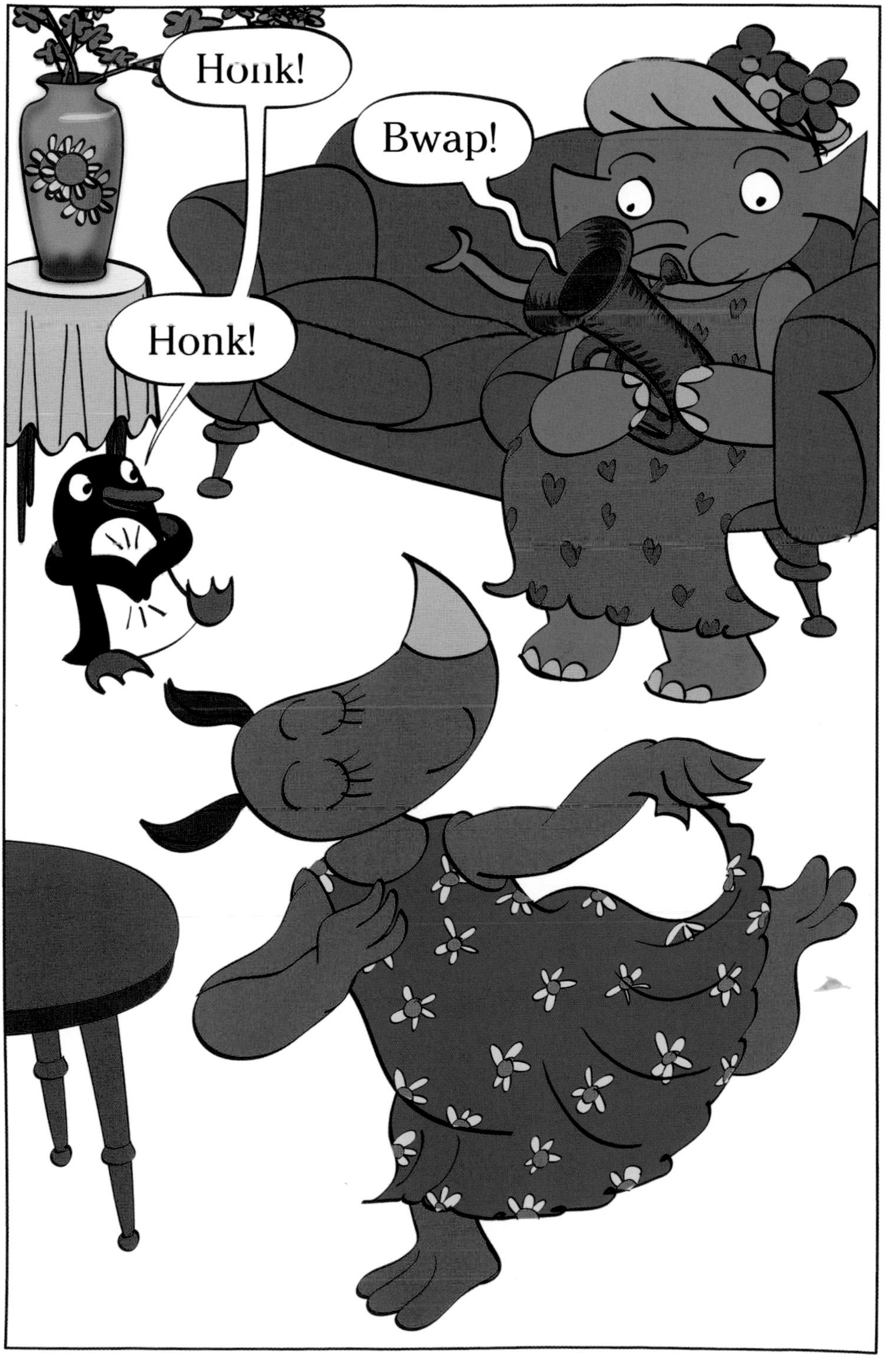
Honk!
Bwap!
Honk!

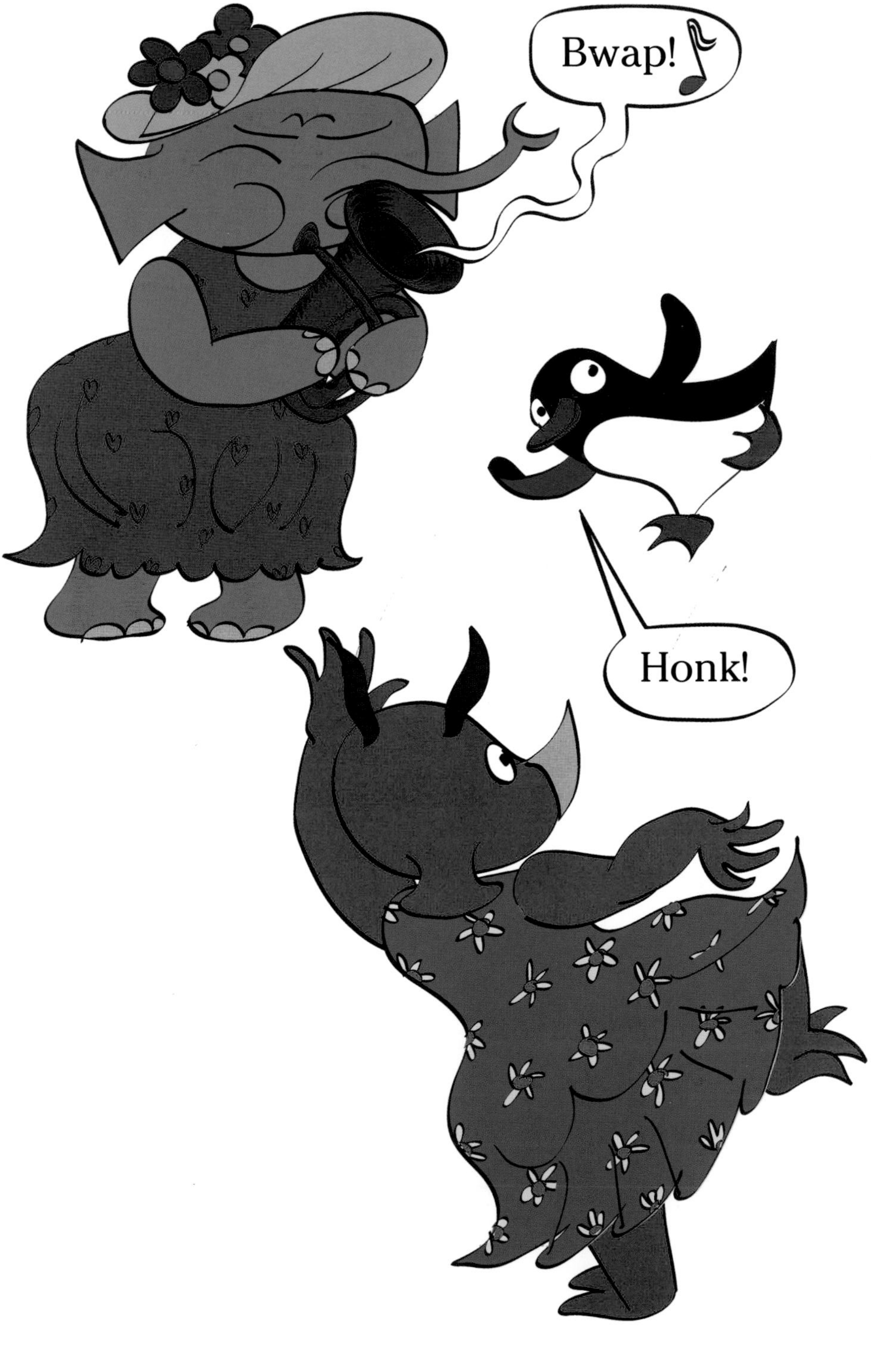
Bwap!
Honk!

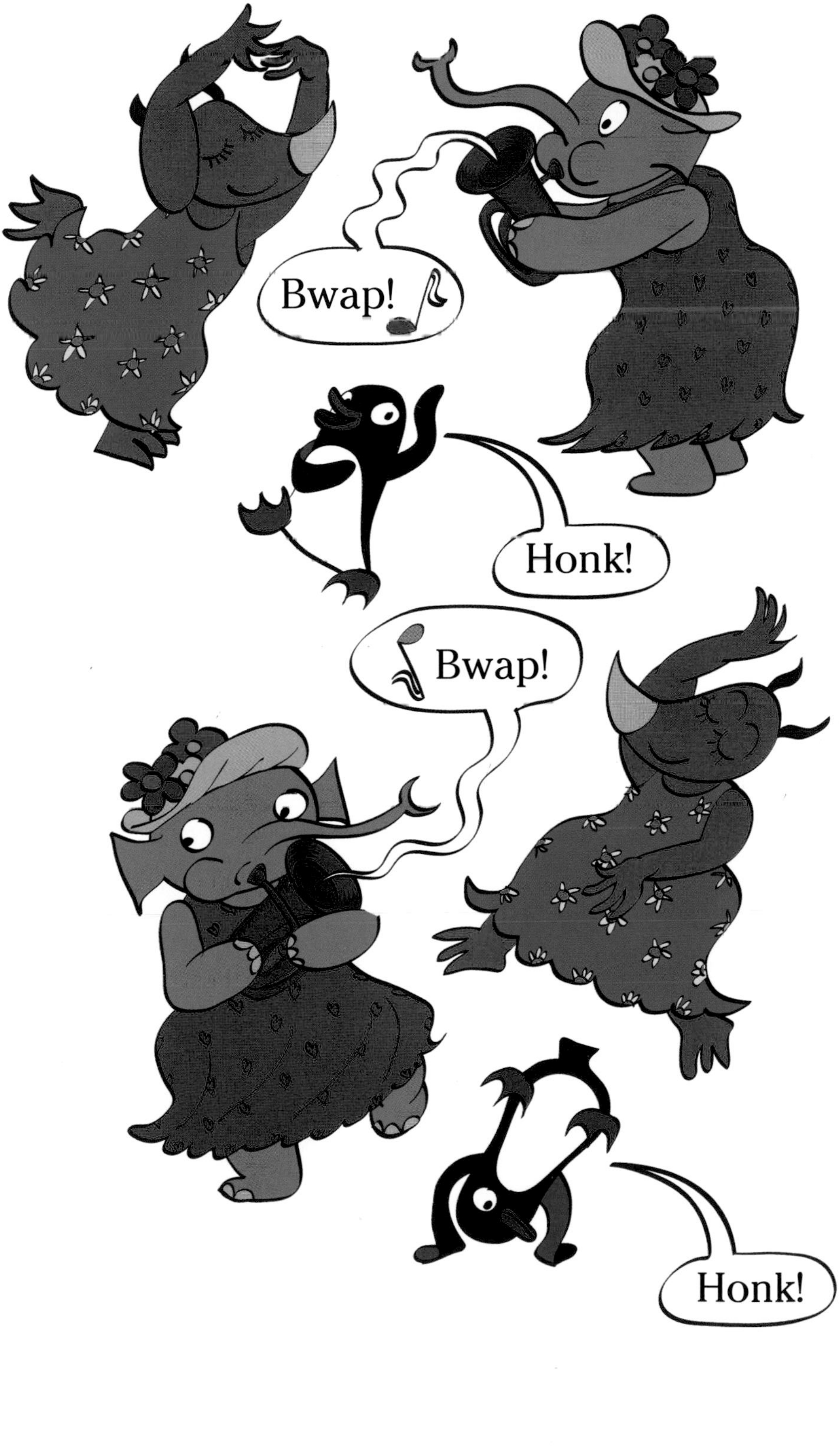
Bwap!
Honk!
Bwap!
Honk!

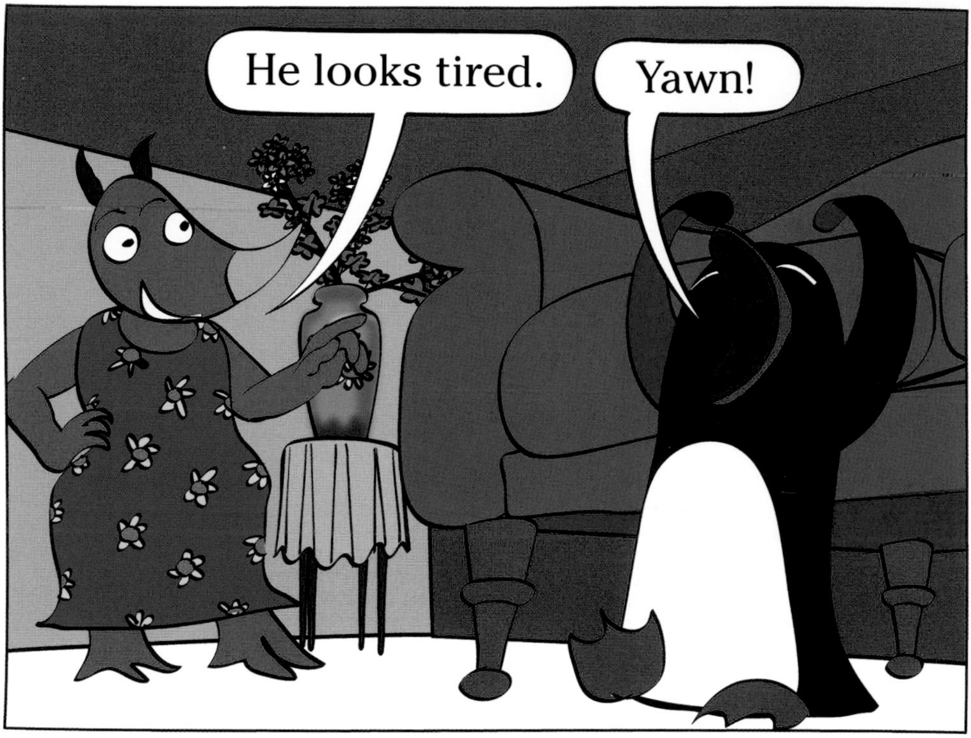
He looks tired.
Yawn!

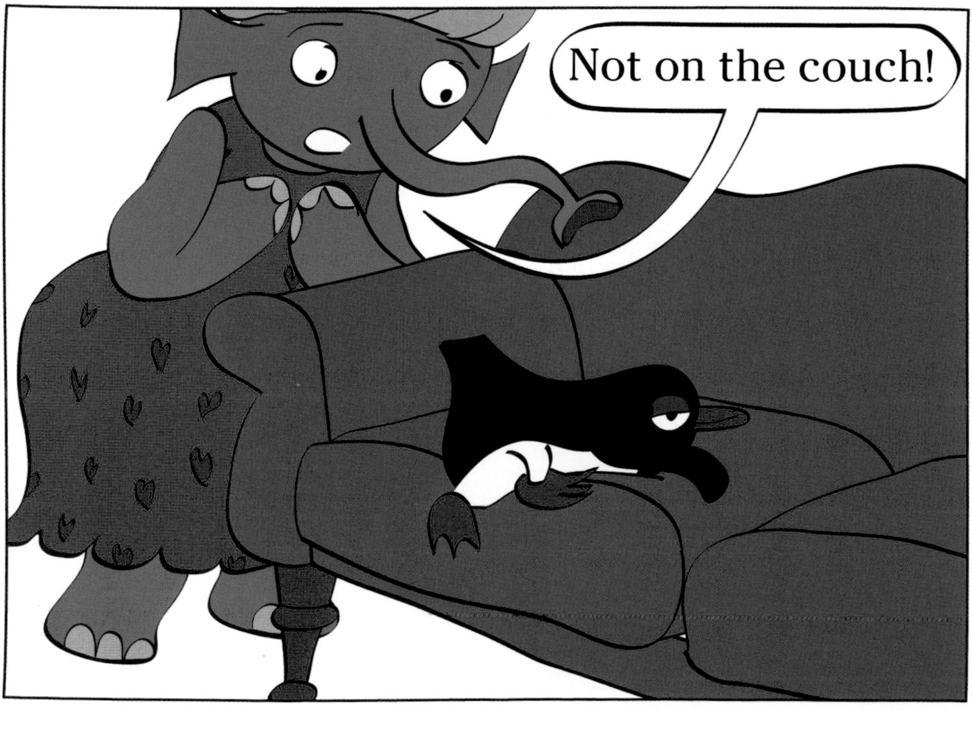
Not on the couch!

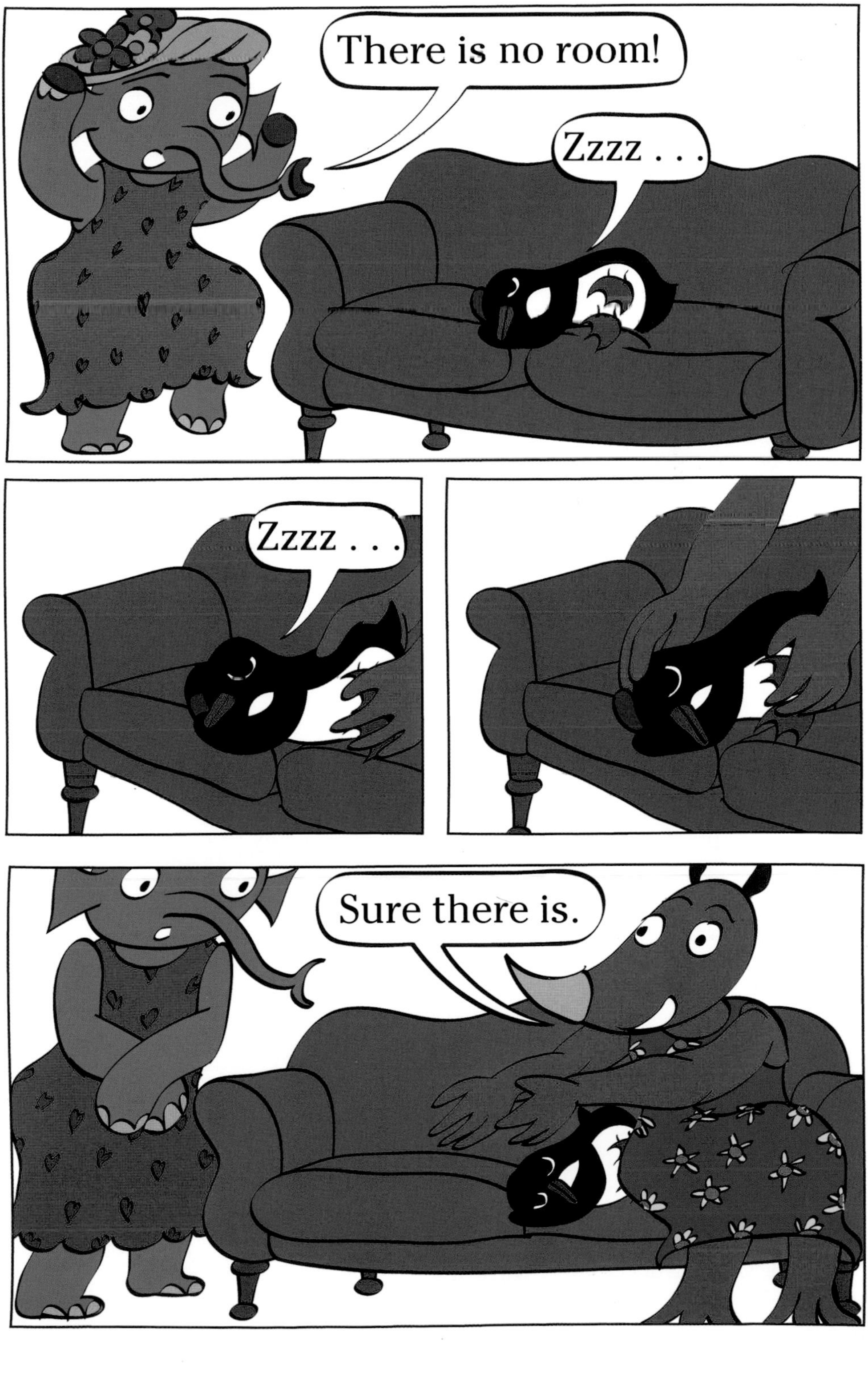
There is no room!
Zzzz . . .
Zzzz . . .
Sure there is.

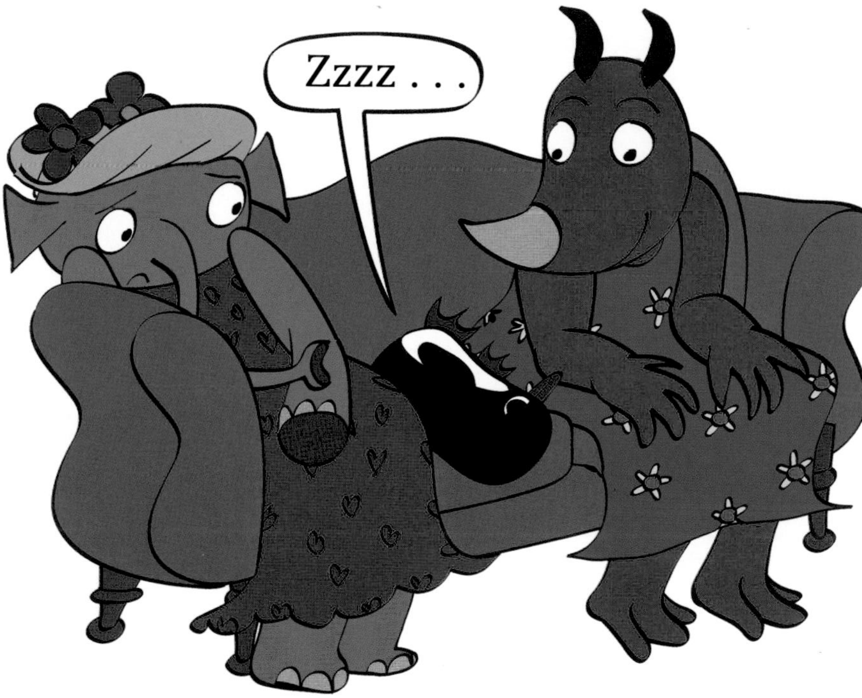
Zzzz . . .

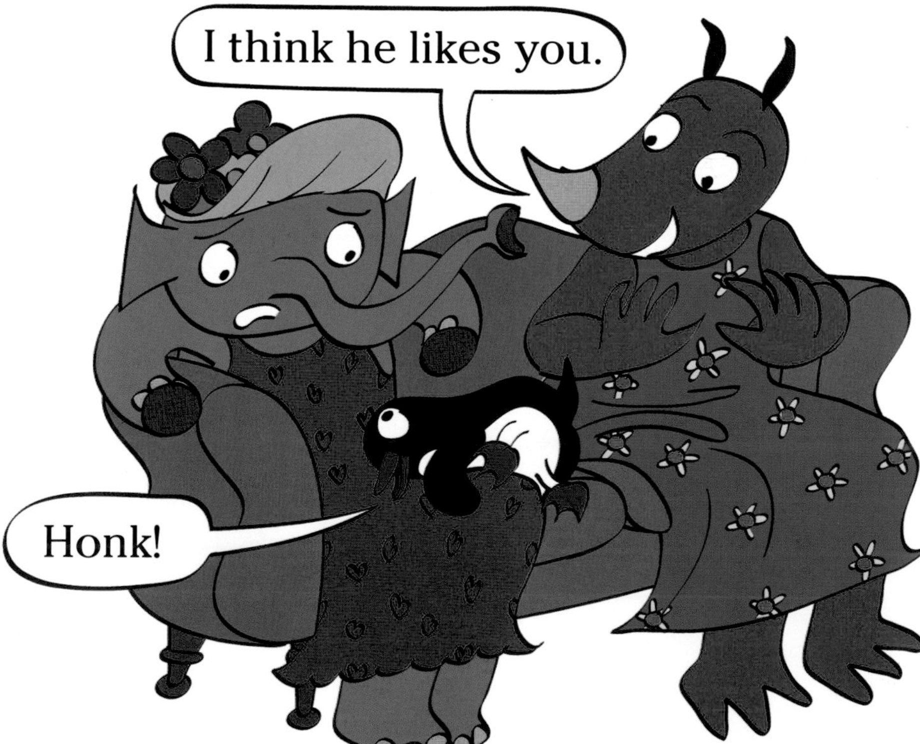
I think he likes you.
Honk!

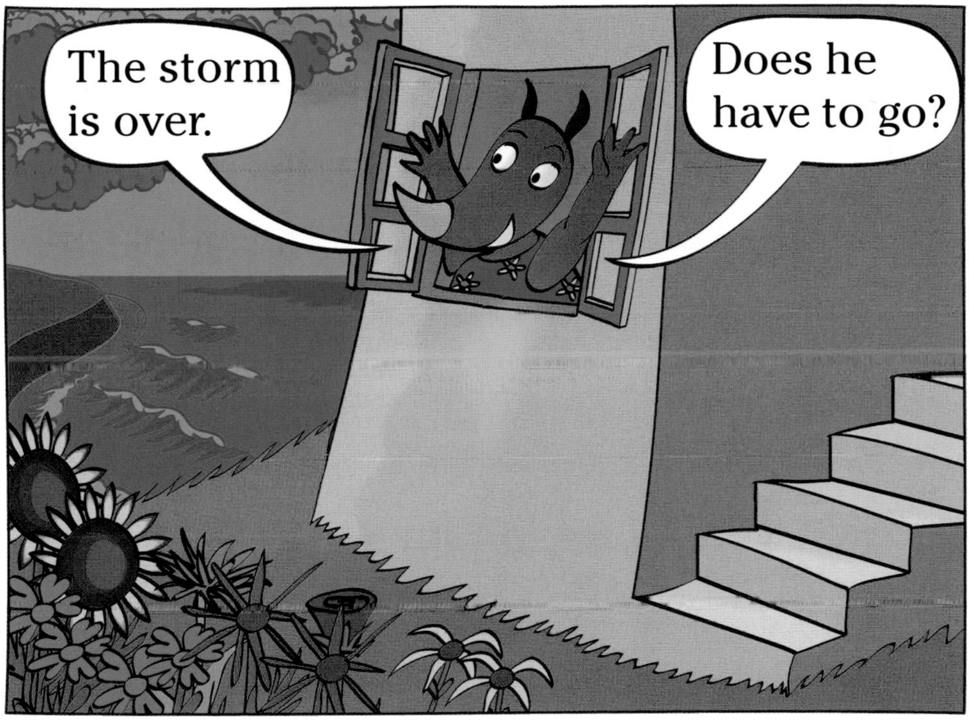
The storm is over.
Does he have to go?

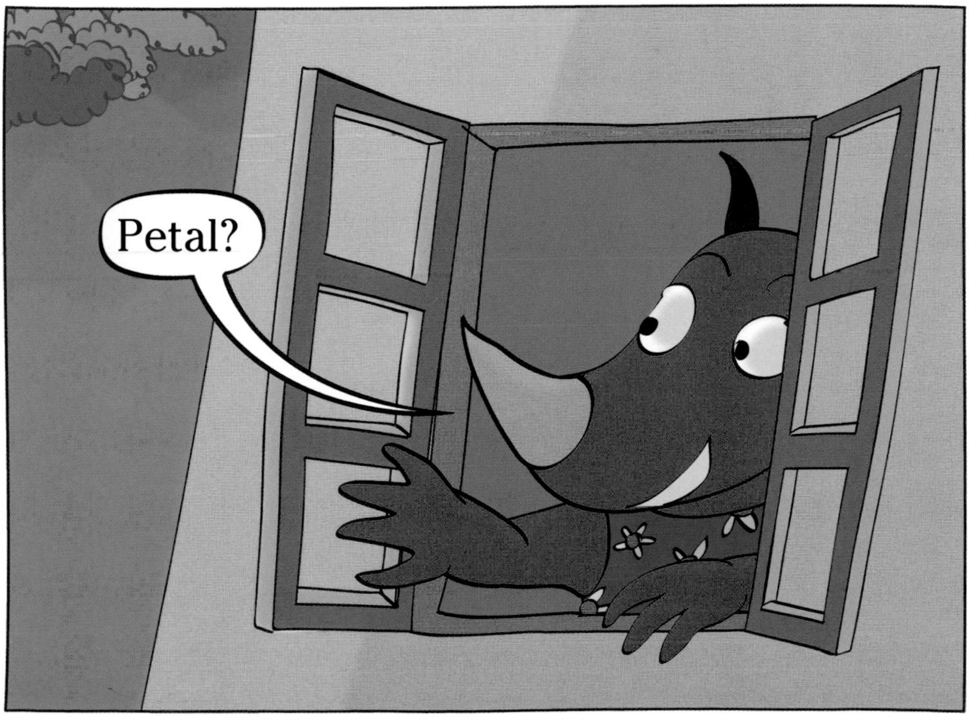
Petal?

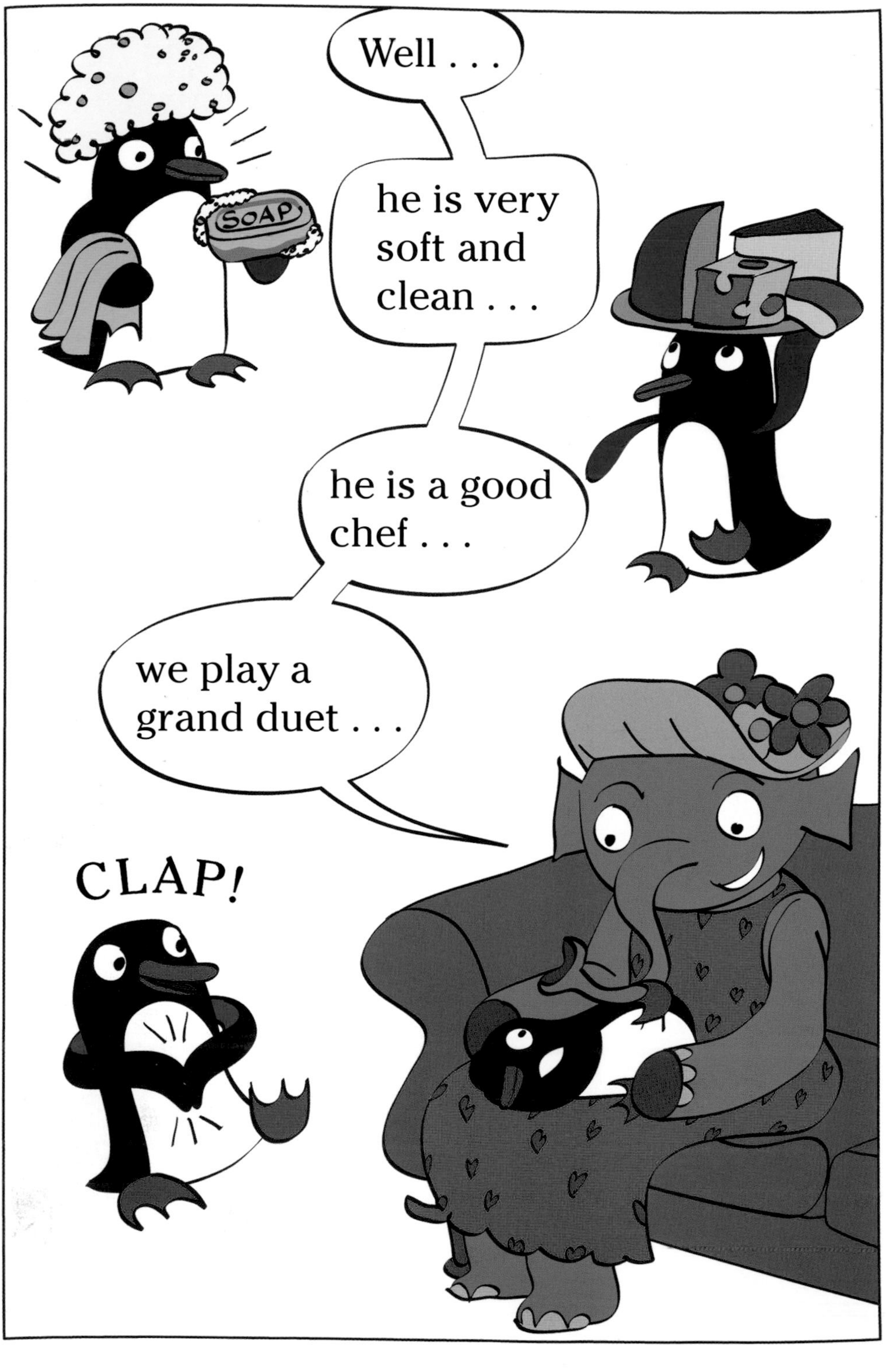
Well . . .
he is very soft and clean . . .
he is a good chef . . .
we play a grand duet . . .
CLAP!
SOAP

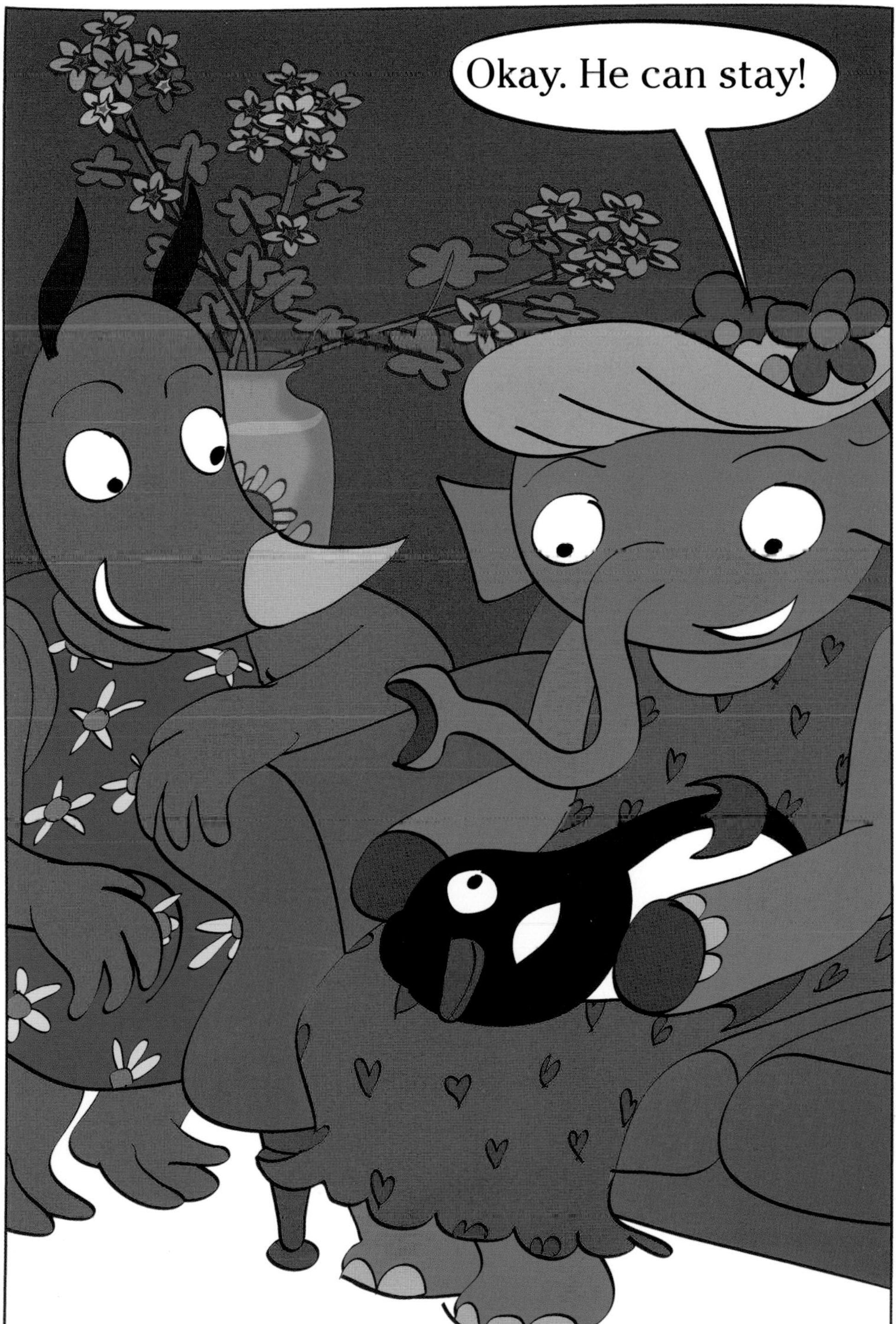
Okay. He can stay!

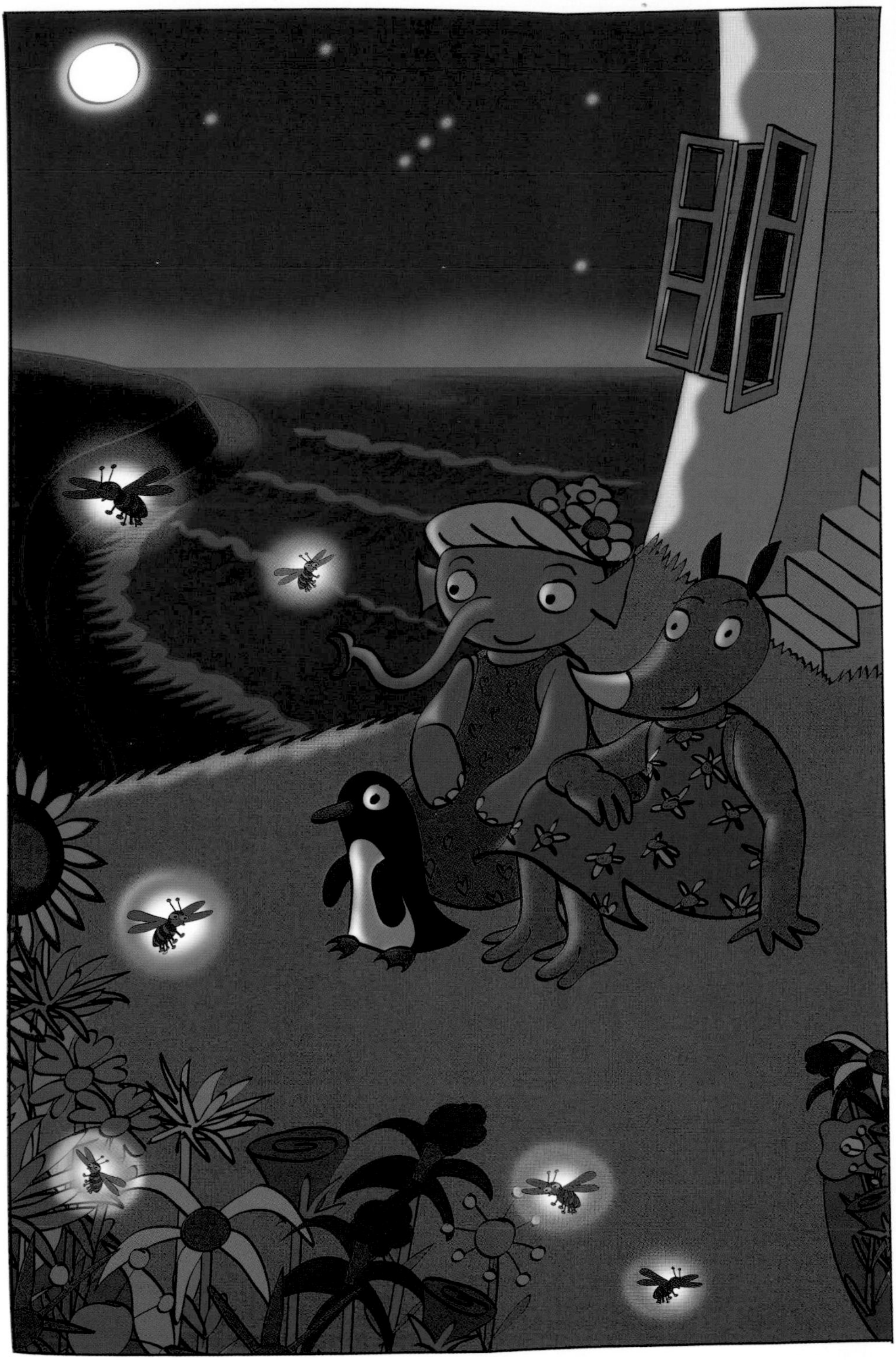